MICHAEL CARRAGHER was born in Newry in 1953 and educated at St Colman's College, Newry, and Trinity College Dublin. After a brief career as a civil servant he became features editor of a national motorcycle magazine before becoming a teacher at the University of Arkansas. He has been writing short stories since 1981 and has been published in the *Irish Press*'s 'New Irish Writing', *Passages*, the *Belfast Review*, the *William and Mary Review* and *The Second Blackstaff Book of Short Stories* (1991). He was shortlisted for a Hennessy Literary Award in 1984 and the Ian St James Award in 1994, and he won the Lily Peter Prize for Fiction in 1996. He has given readings of his work at the Galway Arts Festival and elsewhere.

A World Full of Places
AND OTHER STORIES

MICHAEL CARRAGHER

THE
BLACKSTAFF
PRESS

BELFAST

• A BLACKSTAFF PRESS PAPERBACK ORIGINAL •

Blackstaff Paperback Originals present new writing, previously
unpublished in Britain and Ireland, at an affordable price.

First published in March 1997 by
The Blackstaff Press Limited
3 Galway Park, Dundonald, Belfast BT16 0AN, Northern Ireland
with the assistance of
The Arts Council of Northern Ireland

Reprinted November 1997

Typeset by Techniset Typesetters, Newton-le-Willows, Merseyside

Printed in Ireland by ColourBooks Limited

A CIP catalogue record for this book
is available from the British Library

ISBN 0-85640-595-7

To my sons

*and to their mother
who was good enough
to love me enough
to have them*

Ancient Ireland, indeed! I was reared by her bedside,
The rune and the chant, evil eye and averted head,
Fomorian fierceness of family and local feud.
Gaunt figures of fear and of friendliness,
For years they trespassed on my dreams,
Until once, in a standing circle of stones,
I felt their shadows pass

Into that dark permanence of ancient forms.

JOHN MONTAGUE: 'Like dolmens round my childhood, the old people'

But that was a long time
And no matter how I try
The years just roll by
Like a broken-down dam.

JOHN PRINE: 'Angel from Montgomery'

ACKNOWLEDGEMENTS

Some of these stories have appeared, in various drafts and guises, in 'New Irish Writing', *Passages*, *Superbike*, and the *William and Mary Review*, to whose editors acknowledgement and thanks is hereby given.

Special thanks go to my parents, for their encouragement and assistance. My father's anecdotes and yarns are great story-seed. Without my parents, in any way you care to work it out, this book would never have been written.

The Galway Writers' Workshop was a fortunate discovery; Mary O'Malley, Joan McBreen, Ann Kennedy, Paul Leydon, and Seamus McAndrew were particularly helpful, but I am grateful to all who were involved.

John McGahern gave suggestions and encouragement at one or two critical moments. Larry Brown, my Bread Loaf reader, Richard Bausch, Bob Shacochis, and Bob Ward also helped.

My colleagues and instructors here at the Writing Program of the University of Arkansas take a lot of credit for getting these stories right, some in particular: Gerard Donovan, Tommy Franklin, David Gavin, and David Pratt; Bill Harrison, Skip Hays, Michael Heffernan, Joanne Mescherry, Big Jim, and Brian Wilkie. Thanks, guys – and for the parties too. As the song says, it's great to be part of something so good that's lasting so long.

Finally, thanks go to Tom Harpole, Sandy Johnston, David Minton, and Consuelo Walsh, without whose criticism and constant encouragement I would be writing begging letters.

And to Oisin and Ronan, for suffering my absence.

Contents

Strange sounds from a far-off land   1

Brotherhood   19

Mud and sand   31

The stump and the sapling   40

Coward!   56

A land fit for heroes   74

Underneath the sky   89

Women and men   101

Horns of a whimsical Eden   108

Unconsecrated ground   121

Mad bastards   130

The loanen   139

A world full of places   152

STRANGE SOUNDS FROM A FAR-OFF LAND

PROFESSOR PHELIM McGILLORAY had driven past the Veterans' Memorial in Missoula and was turning into Brooke Street when he heard the banshee. He was so startled that he let the car drift wide. A blare from the horn of a Dodge station wagon sent him swerving back to the right.

McGilloray was horrified, shaking with sudden, awful, pre-posterous fright. Once before he had heard the banshee. He re-membered her cry now, and knew what it meant: his father was about to die. Before the echo of that first cry faded, McGilloray was no longer an academic in an American uni-versity, but a thinly Christianised peasant from the bogs of Ireland, and he knew with certitude that his father was going to die tonight. Just as all in the house had known, one night thirty-three years ago when Phelim was still a boy, that Granda would never see another sunrise.

'Excuse me,' McGilloray said through the window to a passer-by. The man, a young Blackfoot or Lakota in cowboy boots and denims, paused. McGilloray smiled, feeling foolish but needing to know. 'I'm sorry, but, is that a cougar – a lion – I hear?'

'Where?'

The banshee was crying somewhere close at hand, and her cries were penetrating.

'I'm sorry.' McGilloray smiled again. 'I must have been mistaken. Sorry.'

The young man looked at him suspiciously, and walked on.

McGilloray sat in the car and listened for another while, wondering what he ought to do, feeling cooler than he would have imagined. He decided to go home – that was where they'd phone. When he started the engine and drove on, along Brooke and Broadway streets onto Interstate 90, the banshee followed, as she'd followed his family across time – across the world now, too. Just short of Bonner, on Montana 200, she stopped. Abruptly – as McGilloray had known she would.

First thing through the front door he called home. No answer.

Celine was in the front room watching television, the volume turned up high. The canned laughter of the silly sitcom hurt his ears.

'Hello.'

'Hi,' she drawled through an exhalation, without turning. Butts and ashes were scattered on the carpet about the pedestal ashtray, and the room was hazy. McGilloray wrinkled his nose against the stink; but he was polite.

'How did your day go?' He had to raise his voice to be heard.

'Okay.'

Her eyes told him she was drunk again. 'Any – any phone calls?'

'One. For you.'

McGilloray felt light-headed and a little sick. He wanted to grab her and shake her and yell, Why didn't you say so? Why didn't you meet me at the door to tell me? But he just said coolly, 'From home?'

'Nope. A wrong number.'

'I thought you said there was a call for me?' – very sharply.

'That was it. It sounded like the greaser bitch I saw slung around your neck at the university.'

McGilloray ignored the thrust, though he frowned. What was up with *her*? 'I'm having a Jemmy,' he called. He never drank in the afternoons, but he needed something now. Trouble from Louise was the least of it. 'Are you okay?' he asked Celine.

'Top up my vodka.'

McGilloray poured a Jameson into one ice-filled tumbler, vodka into another. He'd call home again as soon as he had this in him. If home didn't call first.

He brought the drinks to the sofa and said, 'Do you mind turning that thing down?'

Using the remote control, Celine reduced the volume by a miniscule amount. She took the tall glass from her husband's hand without a word. Her eyes never left the screen.

'No calls from home?' She was so plastered she might not remember.

'Not unless you moved in with your greaser girlfriend.'

McGilloray took a deep breath. 'If you're speaking of Louise Ramirez, you are speaking of a pupil of mine – nothing more.' Which was strictly true now. 'She may well have had a crush on me one time, but I couldn't help that . . .'

'Oh I'm sure you tried hard, honey.'

'On the unfortunate day you blundered into the dining hall, scattering tables and chairs and slobbering spittle and abuse, making a total show of both of us, Louise Ramirez was upset over a result I'd handed out.' He wished he could have spoken quietly and cuttingly, but the din from the TV was too loud, and he sounded defensive even to himself. As though it was the head of the department he was addressing, in outraged denial.

'Ach spare me the shit, will you!' Celine sneered. 'And get down off your high fuckin' horse. Talk English.'

'My dear, I speak excellent English. I speak it so well people pay me to teach it. But to go on: Louise Ramirez is highly strung. Typically Latin. On the occasion of your campus rampage I was doing what I could to comfort and encourage her on a disappointing result.'

'Well you certainly made her comfortable enough! Honestly, McGilloray, you're such a pathetic worm. Screwing your students in public, and expecting me to believe that bull-shit. Sure everybody knows.' She sniffed scornfully. 'You're going to get fired.'

Jesus, she was one tough old boot. Always had been. He'd known she was strong from the start. Perhaps it was that strength that had attracted him to her – after fifteen years, McGilloray could think of nothing else. It must have been strength, or at least thick wit, that had enabled her to survive being dragged up by the McArdles.

They sat together on the sofa for a minute, in a truculent truce, and McGilloray sneaked a look at her. The image of her father now, she had once been as lovely a girl as her fabled mother, a Dublin society beauty, who had married her father when old Mouth McArdle was still a wealthy man, and all his sons good catches.

Celine caught him. 'A penny for them, Shakespeare?' She was looking at him with that twisted amusement she always feigned when she caught him thinking.

He finished his drink and called home again. There was no answer. Was it all over already? It would be dark in Ireland by now. His father, or Bridie at least, ought to be in the house.

McGilloray went to the kitchen and popped two TV dinners into the microwave. As he waited, he thought about the banshee. He thought about the night Granda died, the funeral, and the consolatory remarks, which had seemed odd even to a child.

'Didn't he get away handy? Man oh man, a lovely death. Not a full day sick. Might have lingered for months, and sure you wouldn't want that. The priest and all before he went. Well-prepared, thank God, and . . .'

There was always something unsaid, the expression of gratitude left hanging, a primeval part of the prayer of thanks not voiced. There had been something, something furtive and unacknowledged even among themselves once it was over, some ritual passed down by whispered word of mouth which didn't reach his ear and might well now be lost, for Daddy would no longer be around to pass it on. McGilloray had never known, could not even guess, what his father had done in the fairy fort on the evening of Granda's funeral.

'What was it you did, Daddy?' he'd asked, years later, when he was old enough to go drinking with his father.

'What?'

'In the fort? After the funeral?'

Hughie McGilloray knocked his whiskey back. 'I'll tell you in a few years. You have to be the same age as Our Lord when he died, to know that.'

'Is it – scary, Daddy?'

'I'll tell you when the time comes.' Mickey O'Neill brought a whiskey and a small shandy. 'But it isn't anything to be scared of, no, son. Good luck.'

'The banshee's scary.'

The old man sipped and paused. 'She is and she isn't. A sudden death might be scarier still, if you found yourself at the gates above, with sins on your soul. Your grandfather was well prepared to meet his Maker, thanks to the banshee.'

The tone sounded on the microwave. McGilloray placed the plates on the table, his thoughts on tomorrow. It would make sense to book the flight now. It would be another gruelling 'covered wagon trip', like the one they'd made to Mammy's funeral: Salt Lake City or Dallas–Fort Worth, La Guardia or Kennedy or Logan – whichever route would bring them home in the shortest time. Eighteen exhausting hours in the air no matter what. Better get it arranged as soon as possible. Start off tonight.

Celine said she wasn't hungry, dammit, so McGilloray sat down to dine alone.

'You ought to watch this, Phelim,' she shouted from the living room. 'It's really up your street.' Laughter burst from a can as though on cue, and Celine cackled.

What an aggravating, fat old sow! McGilloray shoved the plate away from him, his appetite gone.

He thought of calling the travel agent. It was only three o'clock – ten o'clock back home. He called his father instead. The number was engaged now, and he dropped the receiver back onto its cradle as though it had been hot. Chances were, they were trying to contact him.

He went to the bedroom and packed a suitcase for himself. He laid out what he thought Celine might need, though he had his doubts that she would want to come. Or be in any state to do so. Or that he'd want her with him. It was time to end the charade. No reason not to now, with Daddy gone.

Back in the lobby he tried his father's number again. Still engaged.

He stepped out onto the deck, wondering when he'd hear the banshee cry again, waiting for the phone to ring. Celine joined him after a while, barefoot, her empty glass in hand. It was a warm September afternoon, and off towards the Bitter-roots the sun was in decline, casting a cloud-filtered mellowness upon the pines and firs and spruces of the slopes, and the grey-barked cottonwoods along the Blackfoot, their yellow leaves still clinging. There was the reassuring childhood smell of freshly cut grass from nearby, the last mowing of summer for someone.

'Nice, isn't it?' Celine slurred. McGilloray nodded, his mind six thousand miles away. 'Nice place we got here, huh?' She hiccupped and giggled, then got her phoney accent back. 'Hey honey, get me another drink.'

'Get it yourself.'

'Jesus Christ, what's wrong now? It's like living with a bear living with you. Why don't you fuck away off' – she waved an arm at the mountains – 'and hibernate. Give me a few months' peace. Self-centred grumpy bastard.'

'You were spoiled,' Celine went on. 'That's your problem. They all spoiled you. Your grandfather, your father, your mother, your sisters. But not me, buster! Not this kid here. I know you too well. You don't fool me.'

McGilloray shrugged. 'Well, what if I was spoiled? What's it to you if everyone thinks I'm a nice guy? You're right, I suppose, and the rest of the world's all wrong?'

'Yes, they are. They don't know you like I do. You're such a cunning fucker. You made your father feel guilty at keeping you at home, until he sent you to university and ran the farm himself – an old man. But of course then you're so courteous and God-awful grateful! Like the one masterpiece of a letter you write and then forget all about it. So – what's that fancy word you love? So – "politically correct". *Don't call them greasers. Don't call them niggers.* But at the back of it all you're so superior. Your shit doesn't smell, sure it doesn't. And the stupid bastards are so thick they all think you're doing them a favour ...'

McGilloray snapped. 'Who the hell are you calling bastards? Don't you go calling my family bastards. Not *my* family!'

He stared at her until he saw the blush creep up her face. 'Let me tell you something,' he went on. 'I was never unmindful of all my family ever did for me. I knew there weren't enough years left in them, in Mammy and Daddy –' he had to catch his breath and swallow at the realisation that Daddy was stretched out and gasping even at this moment, or that a clot was coursing through his body with an ambush waiting in his brain. 'I knew I never could pay them back,' he went on, shakily, 'so I took all they gave me as a gift – to be passed on' – his voice hard now – 'to the next generation.'

He stared at her. Her chin puckered. 'You're no man. You're no man to cast that up to me.'

McGilloray felt his own face warm. 'Ah Celine, I'm sorry. It's not you – that's nobody's fault. Jesus. Why do we do this to each other? I'm ashamed. Forgive me for that.' He got a lump in his throat, and went on in an unsteady whisper, 'The fact is, Daddy's dying.'

Her expression changed through suspicion to concern.

'How do you know?' She sounded as chastened and embarrassed as himself. 'Is that why you asked about the phone call? Did you get a call at work?'

McGilloray shook his head. Already he was regretting his words. She had scoffed at the banshee legend, and he had never made a big thing of his belief. He had even feigned cynicism – had even wondered if she might be right. But now, despite himself, he told her.

'I heard the banshee. In Missoula. Oh, I know what you think about all that, but you're wrong.' He almost cringed at the jeer he felt sure would come, but she was silent, and he looked off at the mountains. 'There are more things in heaven and earth,' he murmured, 'than are dreamt of in your philosophy, Horatio.'

Suddenly he realised that she was laughing, a wheezy chortle. He felt his face redden.

'Ach would you ever wise up, McGilloray!' she managed, before a coughing fit took her.

'Oh yes, you know everything!' McGilloray had to struggle to maintain a dignified tone. 'Clever people, the McArdles! Oh yes, very clever. Your intellectual uncle didn't have to hire anyone to run his pharmacy when the law looked into his, ah, shall we say, credentials' – he was recovered now, beginning to enjoy this – 'after he'd succeeded in poisoning an unfortunate child? No?' He paused and snickered. 'Good thing there was enough of the old Mouth's money left under the mattress to buy that particular jury, wasn't it?'

'Jaysus Phelim,' she spluttered, 'hold on a minute. Let me laugh! I mean, the banshee. Quite apart from any other bullshit, the banshee only follows *noble* families, to warn them of an imminent demise. So your crowd's definitely off limits to queer old fairy women with nothing to do but sit up all night behind a bush yelling *ochón, ochón.* And don't give me that guff about McGilloray meaning *king.* King bottle-washers in some poor wee shebeen, perhaps.'

McGilloray was speechless. At moments like this, he could kill the bitch and take the consequences.

'I mean, look at yourself, McGilloray. A pompous little hair-dyed asshole who had to emigrate to get anywhere – if an assistant professorship in a two-bit university in the middle of the wild friggin' west is anywhere. Some kings! The McArdles now: now *there's* a noble family.'

'Oh aye. Oh surely.' McGilloray found his voice, albeit too squeaky a one to suit him. 'A bitter race of land grabbers and gombeen men.'

'At least there were no pigs in *our* parlour. At least we had a friggin' parlour. Which is more than can be said for your an-cestral manor, with its leaky thatch and guttery floor. And we had our own banshee – if you were to believe that bullshit.'

'Aha, me lassie, there was more in the pawn than in the parlour at the finish, wasn't there? That's the McArdles for you. Fur coats and no knickers. But big when yous were out, like donkeys' tools.'

The noise of the phone spiked through their rage. Celine's hand flew to her mouth.

In a quick movement, McGilloray stepped through the front door and picked up the receiver.

'Hello?' he choked.

'Phelim?' She made the Irish name sound Spanish: 'Pheleem.'

'Hello?' McGilloray repeated. Celine was standing in the doorway, her lower lip compressed between her teeth. McGilloray squeezed the earpiece tight.

'Phelim, I know what you said. And I respect your wishes. But I have to see you again. Just once. I need to talk to you.'

'I'm sorry, this is the McGilloray residence. You must have a wrong number.' McGilloray hung up, and turned to meet his wife's steely stare. 'Wrong number.'

'The same one?' Her boozy face was flushing with resurrected rage.

McGilloray sighed. 'Let it lie, Celine.' He glanced at the clock. Three forty. Ten forty back home.

'I will not let it lie!' she shrieked. 'Jesus. Will I never learn? You think you can pull the wool over my eyes like I was your mother? With some cock-and-bull story about a banshee? While you're screwing the arse off some bitch with bigger tits than brains? Christ you actually had me worried for a minute. But from now on . . .'

'Oh for Jaysus' sake!' McGilloray roared. 'Will you ever shut the fuck up.'

She was wide-eyed. Speechless. He hardly ever swore.

'You are so fucking special, aren't you,' he hissed. 'Like the seed and breed of you. You're never wrong – oh no. *My father never was wrong in his life.* You know who said that?' he bellowed, over the maddening laughter from the television. 'Your old man. About *his* old man: Mouth McArdle himself. The famous Mouth. Last of the big spenders – on his own fat gut. Sold everything *his* father and grandfather grabbed, and blew it all. Then pawned the furniture in the rented house and drank that too. Then took money from the priest to pay for his operation and blew that in Blackrock, and threw himself in the tide when it was gone.' Her mouth was working frantically and tears were streaming down her cheeks, but McGilloray didn't care. 'And your poor stupid gobshite of a father could say that he never was wrong in his life? Jaysus such a family! Mammy was right to . . .'

She screamed and threw herself upon him. 'I'll gut you, you bastard! I'll take you for everything. See if I don't.'

Her fingernails raked for his eyes. She stripped skin from his cheeks. He grabbed her arms and she snapped at his face. He thrust her away and she came right back at him. A clumsy kick at his groin connected with his thigh. He grunted and punched her, opening his fist in mid-swing to make it a slap, yelled with the pain of what felt like a cracked finger joint as he connected with her temple. She wobbled. Then her eyes rolled up into her skull and she collapsed.

McGilloray sat down on the sofa, sucking his injured finger, trembling and sick. The thought struck him that perhaps this was what the banshee was crying for – the death of his marriage – but he knew that it was a pathetic hope. His marriage had been dead for years.

After a minute he collected himself and checked his wife. She had probably just passed out from drunkenness rather than the blow he'd struck her. She was awfully pale, but breathing almost normally. He struggled to heave her hefty bulk onto the sofa, and left her in the recovery position, in case she might get sick. Then he switched the television off, poured himself another drink, and braced himself to try that call again.

He started when the phone rang. He picked it up – fearfully. Before he got it to his ear he could hear the screaming. Gibberish. Distraught. But – no, Spanish. Oh shit.

'H-hello?'

'Is that the professor?' a woman's voice said in careful, though barely controlled English. In the background Louise was pleading.

'Ah – yes. Who is this?'

'This is Concepta Ramirez. *Mrs* Concepta Ramirez – I am a respectable woman. I am going to destroy you for what you've done to my little girl. I'm going to have you fired. I'm going to sue you for everything you've got.'

'Please,' McGilloray said weakly. 'May I speak to Louise?'

'No! You will not speak to her again. You have ruined her. She is pregnant.'

'She can't be.' McGilloray cast a glance at his unconscious wife and whispered, 'I've had a vasectomy.'

'That too. I am going to sue you for everything.'

McGilloray slammed the phone down, then picked it up at once. Unsteadily, his fingers stepped the hopscotch pattern across the buttons: 00 44 . . .

The banshee howled. McGilloray moaned. In a far-off land he heard the number ringing out. No answer. He croaked a rusty prayer, then dialled again. No answer. Oh Daddy. Daddy. Daddy.

Who could he call? The police? No, they'd treat it as a hoax along the border. The priest? He didn't even know a name. Mary, then – though Mary lived in 'Blayney, twelve miles away. He looked up the number, and called again.

'Hello . . .'

'Dermot. This is Phelim –'

'. . . you have got through to Dermot and Mary Murphy. Neither Mary nor I are in at present, but if you leave . . .'

'Ah Jesus Christ.' Probably at the hospital.

The banshee screamed. Desperately, McGilloray tried his father's number again.

The phone was answered on the first ring. 'Hello?' The male voice sounded hoarse, but strong. 'Hello? Hello!' McGilloray was dumb.

'Hello?' The hoarse, strong voice had an impatient note to it now.

'Daddy?' McGilloray squeaked.

'Hello? Hello, who's that? Speak up. I can't hear you.'

'It's Phelim, Daddy.'

'Phelim? Faylee, lad! How are you?'

'Fine, Dad, just fine!' He paused, feeling confused and even annoyed. 'How are you?'

'Ach not so bad, son, not so bad at all. I've a wee bit of a cold on me, but sure you can't kill a bad thing!' There was a chuckle, then a cough.

'Well, that's good, Daddy. I just called – to see how you were keeping.'

His father hesitated. 'Well, do you know, son, you just caught me going out the door. McCabe called a few minutes ago to see if I'd go with him to O'Neill's. Beat a few hot whiskeys into me, for this oul cold, you see.' A chuckle. 'I was just going down the road to meet him.'

'But Daddy, isn't that rain I hear?' The front door was evidently open.

'Indeed it is, Faylee. It's a dirty oul night. But sure sweet as I am, I'm not sugar. I'll not melt.'

'Well,' McGilloray said reluctantly, 'be sure to wrap up well. Have one for me.'

'I will to be sure, son – if we get in at all. They got awful fussy about closing the door on time. The police have them scalded.'

'Right, Daddy. All the – oh Daddy, I'm sorry, I missed Mammy's anniversary. Celine – I just ordered flowers this morning.'

'That was good of you, son.' Faintly, McGilloray heard a car horn hoot across the world. 'Houl on!' his father called, away from the mouthpiece, the hoarse yell still painful to McGilloray's ear, 'I'm coming.' To the phone then: 'You're a good lad, Phelim. You seldom forget.'

McGilloray felt his face warm. He heard another, longer blast of the car horn far away.

'Listen, Daddy, I'll let you go.' It was an expression he often used in farewell. Now it seemed whimsically apt.

Though maybe not? Daddy sounded grand. Perhaps the banshee had been wrong?

But the banshee was never wrong.

'Daddy! Daddy!' he said urgently. 'Daddy, did you – hear anything tonight?'

'What's that, son?' There was an edge of impatience to his father's voice.

'Oh – nothing, Daddy. Just – any news, like?' McGilloray heard another long blast of the car horn.

'Houl on, ye hoor! I'll be with you in a minute.' Then to the phone, clearly impatient now: 'No son, I heard nothing. I'm as deaf as a post with this oul cold. McCabe was ringing for ten minutes. Only I was stepping out the door just now . . .'

'I won't keep you longer, Daddy. Mickey'll have the door shut. Give him my best, and tell him I'll be in . . .'

'Righto, son. Good luck.'

'Give McCabe my best . . .'

The line was dead.

McGilloray stood staring at the phone in his hand. What the hell was wrong? Was he imagining things? His father had heard nothing; that Indian had heard nothing – and one might think that an Indian, if anyone, would. Daddy was in the pink of health, apart from that cold –

The banshee's final cry split the bright Montana afternoon. McGilloray cursed. Granda had been in the pink of health as well. Just off his grub. Nothing much the matter. But the banshee had cried. And the banshee had been right.

He pressed the cut-off button and dialled international enquiries. Down the hall he heard Celine sniffling and whimpering in the bedroom, a closet door slamming.

'Ah, could you get me the telephone number of the Slieve Brack Inn in Northern Ireland? It would be on the Newry exchange.' He spelled out the names.

He rapped his fingers on the telephone table as he waited. Celine was still whimpering and muttering to herself, banging doors and drawers. Packing. Another scene – but no, she could go. He'd drive her to the airport – or wherever. Give her as much as she wanted – within reason. He had a good lawyer. His marriage was dead.

'Thank you,' McGilloray replied, jotting down the number.

Pressing the buttons, he felt almost foolish. But his father would not scoff. Then he stopped. It would take ten minutes for McCabe to drive to O'Neill's. Longer over wet roads, on a dirty night –

McGilloray gasped. He'd just killed his father! As surely as if he'd put a gun to his head and pulled the trigger. He knew it. He could see the two old men trying to catch up on the crucial minutes lost on the phone, racing against closing time along the narrow streaming roads, in McCabe's battered Fiesta: steering gear worn out, tyres bald as eggs, as likely as not, chassis rotten with rust. He could see them sliding down the Humpy Hill, the worn tyres slipping on the elbow, the rust-bucket crumpling against the parapet of the crooked bridge at the bottom; or over the ditch into the swollen river on its roof. Or maybe at the junction to the unapproved border crossing into Northern Ireland, McCabe switching off the lights to check for traffic from the side, and smashing into another driver doing precisely the same thing at precisely the same time. Or maybe –

It could be anything. But one way or another, it was going to happen. Frantically now, McGilloray pressed the buttons.

'Hello?'

It was a clear line; he could hear the accents of home in the background hubbub and in Mickey O'Neill's voice.

'Mickey! Is my – is Hughie McGilloray there?'

'Hughie? No. Who's speaking?'

'It's Phelim, Mickey. Phelim McGilloray.'

'Phelim, begod. Are you home?'

'No. Look Mickey, I'm sorry to rush you, but would you ever look out and see if Gerry McCabe's car is anywhere in sight.'

'Houl on.'

McGilloray fidgeted and rocked from heel to toe. There was a sense of unreality in this waiting; in listening to those accents so familiar; in seeing in his mind that well-remembered bar-room on a dark autumn night; in hearing pounding Irish rain upon the pavement, while looking out the door upon the arid cheerfulness of a Montana fall, and listening to a neighbour's sprinkler whisper to a parched lawn fifty feet away.

The phone clattered. 'Phelim?'

'Yes, Mickey?'

'Just pulled in.' A laugh. 'Only you called I'd have had the door shut on them.'

McGilloray shivered. Oh Jesus. Maybe it was to be on the way home that McCabe would crash the car, drunk thanks to that second phone call.

'Hello? Faylee?'

'Daddy!' There were tears in McGilloray's eyes. He hesitated, but only for a moment. 'Daddy, I'm sorry to have to tell you this, but I heard the banshee.'

He heard the sharp intake of breath. There was a long, disbelieving silence.

'The banshee?' His father's hoarse voice was guarded, but hoarser than before.

'Yes, Daddy. Earlier today, and again a few minutes ago – the three final screams.' He was crying now. 'Daddy, what can I say to you? Go to a doctor – now. That cold, it isn't just a cold.' He could sense his father's baffled incredulity, his sudden, childish, awful terror. 'And Daddy, Daddy – I'm sorry for ever hurting you and Mammy. I'm sorry for all the times I let you down.' He broke off, overwrought.

His father sighed. 'There son, there now, don't be fretting. Sure you never let us down without making it back up. Don't be crying, Phelim. You're telling me the truth, now?' – sharply.

Unable to speak, McGilloray nodded. His father's voice softened, as though he'd seen the gesture.

'Sure none of us can outrun death. None of us can beat the banshee. And aren't we the lucky family has herself to warn us?' A sniffle down the line; a marvelling, 'Well well well!' repeated after a pause. 'All I can do is make my peace with God. Thanks for warning me, son. I'm as deaf as a post. I didn't hear her.'

'Daddy, I love you.'

McGilloray heard his father's hoarse voice crack. 'Sure I know that, son. Sure I love you too.'

At the core of his breaking heart, McGilloray felt a pearl seed of the purest joy. All the absolution he had craved all his life, even all the forgiveness he'd ever felt it his to return, had been granted by this small word, exchanged for the first time with his father. There was nothing more to say, though he held onto the phone, couldn't put it down. Behind him he heard unsteady steps upon the parquet, the click of a suitcase catch. It hardly registered against this weird peace.

'There's nothing more, Phelim. I'm going to hang up now, son. Make my way up to the priest. Call the house later, if you like. They'll all be there. I'll phone round now and let them know. And Phelim – hello? Phelim?'

Something warned him. McGilloray whirled.

'Hello? Hello, Phelim?' The handset was squeaking on the floor. 'Phelim? Phelim, son? Answer me, son. Son? Oh son!'

'I'm sorry, Daddy.' McGilloray's voice was shaking.

'Son, are you all right? Jesus! Begod my heart near stopped on me there. I thought I heard gunshots.'

'It's all right, Daddy. And Daddy, look: it was all a big mistake. About the banshee. You don't need to worry, you're going to be all right.' McGilloray heard an explosive oath – half anger, half relief. 'You know what it was, Daddy?' His laugh sounded hysterical, even to himself. 'Just a wildcat. That's all. In a trap. The, ah, rancher just put it out of its misery. That's the shots you heard.'

'Christ! Christ you had me worried sick. I was sure I was for the high jump.'

'No. I'm sorry. Sorry I worried you.'

'Right. Good luck. I need a drink.'

'Daddy?'

'Aye?'

McGilloray hesitated. 'The McArdles, Daddy: do you know if a banshee followed the McArdles?'

BROTHERHOOD

THEY PICKED UP THE GUNS in Ned Nally's shebeen after the regulars had gone. Later, just before Jem and Owney left, Ned asked if Jem had taken his oath. The youth felt embarrassed by what followed. The few old men were all half-drunk, and none could remember the words, but between them and Owney they agreed on something while Ned rooted out *The Key of Heaven*, and Jem held the prayerbook in his hand and repeated what they told him, swearing by Almighty God to be true to the Irish Republican Brotherhood. Then all got on their knees and said a decade of the rosary for the new volunteer, and Ned poured a last drink and pledged a toast to the morning.

Through the night Owney talked in whispers while Jem worked. Long ago, a mighty tree had stood here, the biggest in the parish. The biggest in the land, some said. Jem knew the story well, but he listened attentively. An ash, his grandfather had always said it was, but Owney insisted that it was an oak – a poet had said so – the last native oak of Dunreavy Wood, and that its destruction on the Night of the Big Wind was an ill omen for the country: that the conquest was complete; that England had won.

A different bard had taken a different view, and made a song about the wound in the demesne wall opposite, which the tree in its falling had inflicted. Before ivy and weather had covered the repair, the family in the Big House were all dead – of a disease that came from consorting with bad women, Owney said. The Bonds lived there now. The name of the old family was all but forgotten. Owney could not recall it – though Jem suspected that he just didn't try to. Owney knew everything; he had travelled the world.

It had left its mark, that old tree, to this day. Its ripped-up roots had raised a ridge that still remained, incorporated in a hedge, and it was in the ditch adjacent that the two men lay in wait, beneath another tree, a slim young ash, about twenty feet in height – big enough to block the road. Jem had to use the butcher's knife they'd brought, for although the Big House was a quarter-mile away, the sound of a saw or an axe might carry, Owney said, and make the dogs suspicious – the dogs, if not the man. The barrack was close enough for a fast runner to reach it in ten minutes.

Jem's hands soon blistered from hewing and prising out the pale wood chip by chip. But he didn't mind. It was small suffering for Ireland's sake. Owney couldn't take a chance on injuring his hands, for the real job would be done by him. True, Jem had a gun as well, but his was only an old flintlock pistol, and he had never fired it – or any other gun. Owney had loaded and primed it in the shebeen, after setting the flint and checking the spark, and now it lay with the revolver, wrapped in an oilskin, hidden in the ditch, in case a police patrol should surprise them. If that should happen, they would pretend they were drunk. The men in Nally's would swear they'd been there till late. Owney had drunk porter before the toast, and brought some whiskey in a little bottle. At intervals he supped from this. Once he offered it to Jem. Jem shook his head.

'You're better off.'

It was a help on a job like this, though, Owney said. Kept you warm and gingered-up. It wasn't easy to kill a man. Owney had killed loads of men. Mostly niggers of one sort and another. A white man was harder to kill. They had souls. Even Protestants.

From time to time the older man examined the notch in the tree. The original plan had been to fell it in the darkness. That way the landlord's agent wouldn't see it in the morning until he came around the bend. But then Owney said that the dogs might hear it falling, or that Young Bond might miss its out-line when he set out for the town, and take a different route. He was a cute bugger, Young Bond.

He was still called Young Bond, though he was fifty now, or more, and his father long in hell. Jem could remember Old Bond. He'd seen him once, in the tub-trap, with a driver and another man, all grim-faced and armed with sticks. Jem's mother had not had time to grab her little son and pull him indoors, and the child had gaped at the huge white-bearded Antichrist in his long black coat and top hat. Old Bond had glowered back with his fierce red eyes. Afterwards Jem's mother sprinkled holy water on her son, and brought him to a woman who could cure the evil eye.

Young Bond was an even bigger man than his father had been, Owney said, and with an even blacker heart. A danger-ous man. It was said that, like his father, he had sold his soul to the devil. He scorned protection – easy for him, with Satan by his side – and boasted that he could kill ten Fenians without sweating. He travelled alone, despite the troubled times, in a tub-trap or on horseback, without even a driver. Owney said he hoped that Young Bond would not be in the saddle in the morning, for he was an able horseman, and might well jump the roadblock. Owney didn't trust the revolver, an old gun with five shots in the cylinder, and percussion caps. He wished for an American Colt or a Smith and Wesson, which held six brass cartridges and was more accurate. He didn't fancy firing at a moving target with this old thing.

But they had to make the best of what they had. Any gun was hard to get. Even the old flintlock was precious, and Jem felt awed to have been chosen for this task. More than a little frightened, too. But he knew that he was safe with Owney. Owney was the best there was.

A short while before dawn, Owney tested the tree again, and said that it would do. Jem just nodded in the darkness. He was greatly relieved. His blisters had burst, and his blood had made the knife slippery, adding to the difficulty of his task, and his discomfort.

They watched the sky brighten above the Cooley Mountains. Cattle stirred in the field behind them. They heard staggering hoofs, a bovine grunt, and Owney remarked that the American buffalo was the most modest of God's creatures. He had seen them in their millions, but no man any more than himself had ever seen the bull do his business on the cow. They did this in the darkness, like good Catholics.

'Do you know much about all this?' he queried, and chuckled at Jem's silence.

Even brute beasts had more Christian virtue than English Protestants, Owney said. Even Irish Protestants. He spat.

Owney knew everything. He had seen the whole world. He'd served in the British Army in India, and after he'd deserted – a point of pride – he lived with black heathens and cannibals while making his way to Australia. He worked there for a while, then mined in California, made a pile of money and lost it in San Francisco. As he supped from the bottle, he cautioned Jem to have nothing to do with drink or cards or women, then told of crossing the mountains and the prairies, skinning buffalo and driving hide-wagons, with up to ten pairs of mules to a team. He whispered of another Bond he'd known, a man with the strange name Brick, and a strange place without fields or trees called the Llano Estacado, and a big gun called a Remington, a rifle that could kill a buffalo at more than half a mile. He licked his lips and lipped the bottle as he wished for such a rifle now.

The rooster heralded activity. They heard shouts about the Big House, the whinny of a horse.

'God grant he takes the trap,' Owney murmured. He threw the bottle in the ditch.

They opened the oilskin package, and Owney checked the guns. With his thumb easing the cock and the pan emptied, he released the trigger of the pistol and watched carefully the scraping of the flint against the hen. He adjusted the flint a little in the cock's jaws, and reprimed the pan.

'We'll hardly need it, but you never know.' He spat on both guns, blessed himself, and murmured, 'In the name o' God.' Jem blessed himself too, and said the same, impressed by his companion's piety.

Owney wrapped the knife up in the oilskin and put it in a pocket of his coat. They settled down to wait again, Owney impatient now. Jem was afraid. He prayed that the devil wouldn't be with Young Bond in the trap or on the pillion. But he was safe with Owney. He knew that. Safe against anything. Sweat stung the bursted blisters on his palms.

'God grant he takes the trap!' Owney murmured again; then, 'wheesht.'

Jem heard the smart clop of a horse's hoofs. He glanced at Owney. Owney's face was strained as he harkened, his mouth open, his eyes raised slightly. Then he smiled to himself. Behind the hoofbeats was the rattle and creak of harness and wheels.

'Right, *gasún*, up you get there, and when I say push, you

push. I'll leave your gun here – right?'

Jem smiled at that: 'your gun'. He crossed into the field and crouched beside the ash.

The hoofbeats grew louder, but Jem could see nothing around the curve of the road or through the tall leafy hedges. His palms smarted, and the bark of the tree felt rougher than it should. He was dreadfully afraid now, for all his praying and for all his trust. He looked down at Owney. Owney looked tense, the revolver in his hand half-raised.

'Now!' Owney hissed. Jem pushed hard.

He almost cried aloud. His palms slipped on the unfurrowed bark; it seemed as if the skin peeled off. The tree swayed, but only a little. He heard the rhythm of the hoofbeats break.

'Push!' Owney whispered fiercely. Through the bushes Jem glimpsed a horse's white-blazed face, ears laid back on a hog-maned neck, eyes bulging behind blinkers. A huge man was rising in the tub-trap, his bushy grizzled whiskers bristling. A thick arm drew back and down. A whip crack sounded loud, but louder was the bawled command, 'Ged up!'

The cob leaped into a gallop.

'Push, damn your soul!' Owney yelled.

Jem threw his shoulder against the ash. It swayed ... but stiffly, springily resisting. Jem pressed bleeding hands against it. It began to topple – but still so slowly. Owney in the ditch pointed the revolver and fired, the noise sharper than the groaning splintering of wood. The tree was falling now – but far too slowly. Jem leaned forward, unmindful of the agony of his hands, pushing with all his might.

The cob tried to balk, but Young Bond shouted and cracked the whip again. The horse plunged onward, snorting through pink flaring nostrils. Owney fired again.

'You Fenian bastard!' Young Bond bellowed, and lashed the whip at him.

Suddenly the tree broke free. It hinged and kicked backward off its stump. Its butt caught Jem in the belly, knocking him onto his back. He heard another gunshot, branches smashing, squealing.

He forced himself onto his feet. In the road the horse was lying splay-legged, the tree across its back. It was screaming like a tortured Christian.

Young Bond had been thrown into the branches, but already he was free, and leaping down onto the road, roaring like a beast. Owney fired again before the big agent landed on top of him. Jem stared, rigid with terror, and still winded from the blow to his midriff. He saw Young Bond pick up Owney as though he were a child and shake him. Owney was crying. He'd dropped the revolver.

'Fenian bastard.' Young Bond said through gritted teeth. 'Fenian bastard. I'll hang you.'

He banged Owney's head against the fallen tree. Jem saw Owney's eyes roll up towards the sky, his eyelids flicker. He heard Bond laugh, saw Bond shake Owney again until Owney's eyes opened wide. But Owney didn't seem to know what was happening. His hands came up and pawed at the thick wrists, but with a feebleness that put Jem in mind of his baby brother scrabbling at his mother's breast. Young Bond's big fingers were clasped about Owney's throat. Owney's face was turning red.

'I'll see you hang, McQuaid!' Young Bond shouted. 'You and that wee O'Hanlon skitter in the field!'

Jem flinched at the sound of his own name. He drew a deep breath, and moved. Stealthily, he crossed the hedge. He stooped, picked up the flintlock, pointed it at Young Bond's back, and pulled the trigger. Nothing happened. Urgently, but chastened now, he lowered the gun. He hauled the cock back and thumbed the hen, mindful not to spill the powder from the pan, or to dislodge the flint, as Owney had cautioned. Carefully he aimed, with one hand on the grip, the other steadying the barrel. Remembering Owney's instructions, he held his breath, and gently squeezed the trigger.

The gun jumped like a live thing startled in his hand. Through a cloud of smoke he saw blood burst red on Young Bond's neck, more spray from his mouth onto Owney's face. He felt faint warmth in his flayed left hand. He saw the big man stumble against the fallen tree.

But still Young Bond held Owney by the throat. Still he stayed on his feet. The tree was lodged on the field wall at between chest and waist height, and Bond had Owney bent backward across it. Owney's face was purplish under Young Bond's blood. His eyes were big like a frog's. Jem crept up behind the agent, and hit him on the head with the pistol barrel. Young Bond made an animal sound through clenched teeth. He jerked an elbow behind him, and lashed backward with one foot. But he never loosened his grip on Owney's throat. All the time the horse was crying, the steel of its hoofs scraping on the metal of the road. The noise made Jem want to drop the pistol and cover his ears. The air was thick with the smells of gunsmoke and horse shit. Jem was breathless and dizzy with it all, getting sick in his stomach. His strength was leaving him. Half-heartedly, he struck again at the head of the landlord's agent.

Owney was limp now. He slipped along the tree and down, bringing Young Bond into a stoop. Still Young Bond held on. Jem dropped his weapon. He took a deep breath, then another, fighting down the urge to flee. He grasped the broad shoulders and tried to pull Bond off. It could not be done. It was Satan he was fighting, and the devil could not be killed. He'd strangle Owney, and then he'd turn on Jem. Jem released his hold, and for a moment stood there, looking wildly about. He backed off a step, then two. He cast an anguished look at Owney.

Owney's tongue was sticking out. His frog's eyes stared at Jem, imploringly. Jem lowered his gaze. Ashamed of his cowardice and his near-betrayal, he picked up the pistol again, reversed his grip, and flailed two-handedly with the thick, iron-bossed butt, again and again and again.

With the same reluctance as the tree, Young Bond fell onto his knees. But still his fingers were locked on Owney's throat. Jem battered on the back of the grizzled head. Blood was seeping through the hair, splashing with every blow. Jem's face was wet with it; his hands were slippery again. He was sobbing with exertion, whimpering with horror. He felt and heard the skull give way.

Young Bond collapsed. His thick fingers lost their grip. Jem dropped the pistol again and heaved the big man off Owney. Owney gasped, an awful fleshy sucking noise. He turned upon his side and vomited. Jem raised him up, with his hands under Owney's armpits. With Jem's help, Owney raised himself onto his elbows, and shook his head. He rolled onto his back and lay there beside Bond, shuddering and wheezing. His face, where it showed through Bond's blood, was greenish now. Jem glanced at Young Bond, who looked to be dead but for his eyes. His whiskers and the front of his shirt were drenched in blood. There was red froth about his mouth. His forehead was waxy white. The horse was screaming. Its front feet, on the far side of the tree, were scrabbling like a swimming dog's, its hind legs on this side were splayed, tremoring. Jem covered his ears, shut his eyes, and howled.

Owney's weak voice shamed him. He tugged Owney to his feet, staggering under the weight of him. Owney was as pale as the dying man, his eyes cowed. He swayed against the fallen tree, and retched again. He retched for long after nothing came up, for long after Jem was shouting silently at him for the two of them to be far gone from here.

'The gun.' Owney's voice was a whisper, painful even to listen to. Jem could hardly hear. The horse's noise was piteous. 'The gun!' Owney signalled urgently. 'There's one shot left in it.'

He dropped to the ground, crawled under the tree, and set off down the road at a swaying run.

Jem found the revolver in the grass. He went to where Young Bond lay on his back. Young Bond was breathing shallowly, with long moments between each breath. With every breath, blood bubbled in his nostrils. His eyes were glassy now, but there was a fierceness in them still – the same fierceness that Jem remembered from Old Bond's eyes. He glanced across his shoulder, fearing to see something with a tail and horns, horrible to behold. He shivered, and crossed himself. For a moment he stayed bent over the fallen man, the gun like the weight of a mountain in his hand. He thought of the Act of Contrition, but was not sure if it might not be a sin to say it for a Protestant.

Then he stooped beneath the fallen tree, and went up to the horse. He held the revolver to the white-blazed face and fired. The gun rocked upward in his hand. The horse stopped crying. Its jaw cracked against the road. Its front legs quivered, and were still.

Jem threw the gun into the ditch. Faintly, he heard voices calling about the Big House, the thud of galloping hoofs. He turned and ran off after Owney. He ran for half a mile before he caught him up.

'What kept you?' Owney gasped, not breaking stride. 'Christ, if they catch us we're done!

'The fields,' he said then. 'Take to the fields. They'll be following the road.'

They ran until they came to a hazel copse beside a stream.

They flopped onto their bellies and slurped like animals. Owney rolled onto his back, his chest heaving. His face was flushed and wet. Young Bond's blood was washed away.

'Son of a bitch near killed me,' he panted, staring at the leaves. He gave a short, high laugh. 'You finished him?'

Jem hesitated. 'I shot the horse.'

Owney jerked to face him. 'The horse?'

'I couldn't leave him that way,' Jem murmured.

'The horse?' Owney's eyes were wide, his face filling with anger and alarm. 'You shot the bastardin' horse? With the last shot we had?'

'I couldn't leave him that way.' Jem could feel his own face flush.

'No, but you could leave Young Bond! To hell with the horse. The horse couldn't hang us.'

'He was dying, Owney. He was breathing for death. He was done for.'

'But he was still alive. And you heard what he said. He saw the pair of us. He could hang us both. If he breathes a word to anyone – oh Christ, *gasún*, why didn't you shoot him?'

'I couldn't leave the horse that way,' Jem repeated, full of shame.

Owney's eyes blazed at him. Then he looked at the hazel leaves. His lips were working. Jem heard shreds of the Hail Mary.

Owney sat up. He fumbled in his coat pocket. He brought out the oilskin package, unwrapped the butcher's knife.

'Here.' He thrust it, handle first, at Jem. Jem hesitated.

'Take it,' Owney shouted. 'It's your mess, you clean it up. Take it!'

Slowly Jem reached his hand.

'You'll be all right.' There was an anxious sort of a smile on Owney's face. 'There's loads of time. They'll run to the barrack first. Take them half an hour. They won't go down there by themselves. They'll be afraid. They're all our own sort anyway, bar the missus and the brats. They'll take their time.'

Jem remembered the urgent calls and hoofbeats from about the Big House as he had started his run. But his hand was closing on the knife's haft. It was sticky with his own blood.

'Good man. Good man. I'd go myself, only the son of a bitch near killed me. You know that – don't you, Jem? I'd go myself. But you're young. You weren't hurt, like I was, Jem. You're young and in your health. I can hardly walk, Jem. You'll be there and back inside five minutes.' His eyes locked with Jem's for a moment. 'You'll be there and back inside five minutes. You won't get caught.'

Jem stood up slowly. Something must have shown in the face he turned to Owney.

'Aw Jem, son, don't look at me like that! Sure I'd go myself, only I'm the way he has me. You wouldn't doubt me – sure you wouldn't? But you go back. Go back now, like a good chap. Go back and finish it. Stick that blade between his ribs, Jem. Split his black heart. He'll hang us if you don't.'

Jem turned and started walking.

'Hurry up,' Owney urged behind him. Jem kept walking.

'Oh hi!'

Jem turned. Owney had crossed the stream. His face was wicked as he warned: 'If you're caught, you don't know any names. You took your oath – remember? You're in the Brotherhood. You won't forget. You won't forget your oath. It was you that done it, anyway.'

Mud and sand

THEY FACED EACH OTHER across the bars of the corral, not quite as equals but with something akin to respect. Something like wary insouciance – though it was in the mind of the man to get rid of the beast. He was getting cranky in middle age.

The man leaned with beefy forearms stretched along the top rail, square chin resting on the backs of hairy hands. Worker's hands, hardened and broadened and battered and scarred by a lifetime of grubbing a living from the soil, wresting a shilling from the fists of sharp-eyed, sharp-witted dealing men in mart rings and public bars. Thick stubby fingers and nails like a badger's claws, which were seldom clipped but wore down through hard use, and were usually a little overlong, though never broke or split. Strong nails. Strong hands.

Everything about the man denoted strength: the hands and arms, the Neanderthal neck and massive torso, the short but hypertrophic thighs. Every year he washed his face a little farther back, but the hair that was left to him was wiry and still red. That he was past his prime was a thought that seldom crossed his mind, and never stood in his way. He lived as generations before him had lived, as beasts had before them, and plants before all. He survived through persistence, unwitting self-confidence, a creed and faith instinctive more than learned; a primitive organism's blind grip on the earth, of which the organism might appear almost an offshoot. 'All balls and no brains', someone had once described him, and the man, hearing of this, had not been displeased. If he wasn't as smart as some of the lads he'd gone to school with, he was as cute as a bread-bin rat, and the cuteness had fed him fat. He got by. He made out. He did all right. He had a well-stocked farm and dry cash put by when many of the same smart lads had gone bust or would be working for the banks for the rest of their lives; all men who had sneered at his animal wariness and human contempt. What could bank men in their white shirts ever know of farming?

The evening's work was almost done. All the cows had been milked. There only remained to separate the blue-roan shorthorn for sending to the meat factory. She'd come-round again today. The rest of the herd had been in calf for months now. He dried them all off towards the back end of the year to have them calving-down in early spring. It made no sense to feed a barren old shorthorn through the winter; she'd only keep the sap up in the bull. Shorthorns' day was over anyway. Even the man, suspicious of change as that bread-bin rat about a trap, had replaced most of his with piebald Friesians, though he retained the Angus bull, all but a living relic now of days when cattle were red or roan or black, and small and hardy.

The sun was going down and autumn's chill bit into the air; there would be an early frost. But it was still quite bright and would not get fully dark. The skies were clear, and a harvest moon was abroad.

The thought brought the bull back to mind. He would have to watch his step. It was a dangerous time of year. Even mild-mannered bulls were known to turn wicked at harvest time. Every year some man in Ireland lost his life to a bull, and every year it happened in late summer or early autumn. It had always been thus. The man did not wonder why. That it occurred was all he needed to know. And he had been careless of late: the chain that normally dragged from the nose ring and would get in the way of a head-down charge had broken off and been lost, and he had not yet replaced it.

Perhaps he should replace the bull. Or just get rid of it and keep no more; sell it to the factory with the old cow. It made little sense to keep a bull to service his middling-size herd when few neighbours now bothered with the long trek up the loanen with their heifers and milkers. The AI service was handier, and hardly more expensive, and carried less risk of brucellosis. He might start to use it himself. 'The bull with the collar and tie' – he had sneered at the notion of an AI man when the service had first become available, but time and the thought of money had nibbled away at his mistrust.

Time, too, had changed the milking yard, which a town-dwelling cousin who watched Westerns in the cinema had long ago nicknamed 'the corral'. But the name had stuck. Railway sleeper uprights had been replaced by girders, to which were fastened rails of steel in place of seasoned ash. Life had changed. No townie cousins came on holiday. The farm was a lonely place now. Brothers and sisters, all ten who had lived, were scattered like chaff across England and America. They had not visited since the mother's funeral. A card at Christmas; the occasional letter bearing news of domestic sorrow or joy that could only mean little or less to a bachelor farmer. The dog was his only companion, and a faithless enough and shallow one, more a casual acquaintance than the man's best friend. It came and went as the humour took it, and might be gone for days if there was a bitch in heat. Though not one to brood on mysteries, the man did sometimes wonder at the companions of his world, and their odd hierarchies. The meanest cur that would cringe at a harsh word might put manners on the bravest bull.

He did not have a woman. He'd never had. But unlike many in his place, he did not waste time in yearning like a sappy young spike for a life that could never now be his. Desire had gone to seed without ever bearing fruit or having flowered. The mystery of sex had been jaded in a lonely bed, its fascination soured as the yellowed sheets, and he had drunk with enough to know that he was not the only virgin-man of fifty in the world, married or single. No longer did he envy his bulls their lives of lustful leisure.

The coal-black brute across the gate met its keeper's gaze without hostility. With indolent curiosity, perhaps, if it was capable of sentience. All balls and no brains. If the expression ill became the man, it almost served the beast. The appendages that were all but redundant in one justified existence in the other – though now it ate as much as it was worth. At less than a ton it was a veritable midget beside the upstart Continentals of the AI station, but for an Angus it had gone to fat; not so much that its usefulness was compromised, but middle-age spread was there. The barrel body was obese, and made the stubby legs seem almost comical. The hump above the broad shoulders and thick neck denoted strength, but it was a strength that had been sapped by advancing years and the softness of domesticity. Behind the solid wall of skull there lurked an organ that would seem to register instinctive urges only. If animal emotion ever sprouted, it had never swelled here. Even fear had been consigned to fits of fright, when hoofs were being pared or at drenching or injection. Emperor of eighty acres, it was a lethargically jealous suzerain. A primitive survival drive controlled the torpid champing of its jaws and the thrusting of its loins, and occasional head swing at a ruttish yearling. But something more than instinct's urges glowed and sometimes fired in the murky pathways of its brutish brain.

The man too was a stranger to fear. He'd found his place in life, or had accepted that accorded him. He had grown beyond insecurity and had yet no need to worry about infirmity. But his courage was grounded in confidence, his confidence in caution, and it was caution that made him lift the stick when he entered the corral to separate the roan cow. A few good wallops of an ashplant to a calf, like kicks to a pup, were not forgotten, and could make a grown bull, even a temperamental bull, back down at the sight of a stick.

But complacency intruded for a critical few seconds. The bull backed away from the opening gate and the man disarmed himself. The chain, the nose-ring chain he should have replaced, was his undoing. He saw the dull glint of its links embedded in the trampled mud and dung, and dropped the stick to haul it out two-handedly. Yet things could have turned out worse. Had the animal charged a second sooner, the man would have been knocked from his stoop headfirst to the ground; a second later and his spine might have been snapped by the impact. As it was, he was almost erect when the blow to his backside hurled him across the yard, violently, but on his feet, the chain grasped with the unthinking tenacity of a drowning man.

He realised immediately what had happened, and when he was pitched against the bony bulk of the blue-roan shorthorn he ran to place the cow between himself and the second charge he knew would follow. The crush pen was only a few yards away – too far, he saw at once.

The second charge connected with the cow's hindquarters even as the man was scurrying behind her. With a bawl she leaped away, leaving him exposed. The bull, as though acknowledging a rival, paused to snort and paw the ground; the man swung the chain. But it was a clumsy defence. The blow bounced off the armoured skull and heavy neck, served to infuriate rather than intimidate.

Where was the stick? Where was the dog?

But before he could draw breath to shout or whistle, the bull charged again, black as a secret sin in the dying day. Its eyes, until they closed before the impact, looked bereft of passion, all but mild. The man was hit in the midriff, but this time was prepared, with heavy belly flexed against the blow, thighs tensed to leap with it. The bull ran on, propelled by instinct and momentum, the weight on its head and neck no encumbrance. But the man had instinct too. By wrapping his arms about the huge neck in an unnatural embrace, and shifting a little to one side, he was able to bury yellowed canines and incisors in a steel-tagged ear, roaring caveman anger through clenched jaws with such breath as remained in him.

The animal broke stride. It tossed its head. The man was flung to the ground – near the crush pen – so near. But before he could move the, bull was upon him, dropping on its knees to gore, its massive skull against the man's breastbone. The man felt his chest being emptied like a squeeze-box. His vision darkened, narrowed to a tunnel that was quickly filled by a blacker bulk. He got a glimpse of the hind hoofs slipping as the animal sought purchase in the viscid dirt. Then even the vision of the black bulk faded against total darkness. And suddenly the man knew fear.

It was an odd fastidiousness that reprieved him. The bull raised its head to draw a breath, then a ragged snort blew thick grassy saliva in its victim's face. In the momentary respite, the man's lungs had filled like a blacksmith's bellows. His next reaction was disgust. As his strength waxed, however so little, he raised his hand to wipe the slobbery mess from his mouth, and his knuckles brushed the nose ring.

At once his fist clenched on it. He twisted. The bull reacted. There was no weight upon the man's chest. His lungs sucked hard again. The dark tunnel returned to view and its vista widened. But the chest pain remained: not crushing suffocation now, but a stabbing in the ribs that sharpened as his lungs filled. But vigour was back now, and pain served to sharpen his aggression and to feed hostility. Hatred found a place, and gave reinforcement to the groping thrust of his free hand as he drove a steely-taloned thumb into the soft and yielding tissue of the deadpan eye.

The explosive bellow was muffled by the man's grasp on the bull's muzzle. The beast shook its head to rid itself of its suddenly unbearable burden. But the man, motivated by instinct to hold fast onto his only straw, as well as by revenge, twisted harder on the ring and dug his thumb more deeply into the eyeball, until his nail grated against the socket wall. His hand was slippery with blood, which ran down his wrist to puddle in the elbow of his jacket, and dribbled over his face. But squeamishness was far from mind now. The bull's bass bawls rose in pitch, betraying fear as well as pain. The tossing of its head took on the random pattern of panic, and panic's strength. It broke its toreador's hold, and flung him high into the air.

The fall winded the man again, and his ears sang from the head blow he'd received. He had landed sitting against something that was hard and cold against his head, though the back of his neck was warm. He realised that he had hit one of the girder uprights of the crush pen, and that it was his own blood that was warming him. He knew that he had only to roll beneath the rails to find a refuge, but this puny effort was beyond him. His vision was spangled and out of focus. He couldn't even see the bull. But he had landed on its blind side.

The animal was rampaging around the corral, tossing its head as though still trying to rid itself of the torture. It roared continuously, a throaty din like the noise of a beast of prey. The cows huddled in a corner unheeding, calmly back-chewing. Twice the bull passed within six feet of its erstwhile victim, apparently unmindful. But when movement returned to the man and he moved to roll into the crush pen, the bull broke into a charge.

Only the muzzle struck him this time, and it served to shunt him under the bottom rail into safety from the onslaught that would have smashed the wooden rails to matchwood years before. The steel tubing bent but it held, and the animal eventually tired.

The man lay quietly, not trying to get up, breathing shallowly. That way it didn't hurt so much. He raised a hand to rub the mud and blood and mucus from his face, gasped at the twist of pain, realised his arm was broken. A fit of coughing shook him, and he shut his eyes against the agony, but not before he had a vision of dark droplets against the pale horizon, blood blasting from his throat to fleck the rails. His clothes were soaking. He was chilled by shock and inactivity. His teeth began to chatter.

The harvest moon rolled across the empty sky, replacing twilight's gloom with an eerie luminescence. It imparted a ghostly glow to the white-patched hides in the corral.

The man forced himself to stand, hauling himself up by the rails, hand over elbow. Not a cloud to hold a bit of heat; just a few useless stars, and a wide bright halo round the moon. 'The man in the moon is training his colt,' the old people would have said. He hadn't heard that queer old saying in a wheen of years.

He was marooned, as his cousin might have put it long ago.

The crush pen opened front and rear into the bull's domain. But the bull was a prisoner too, at the mercy of thirst and hunger and the ruin of its eye. Later the animal might sleep, and the man might get away – if he could stay awake, and find the strength to move. Tomorrow the lorry driver from the meat factory should come, or the unabated bawling of the unmilked herd might bring some distant neighbour to investigate. But what would such a neighbour find? Already it was freezing, and it was hard to hold himself on his feet.

They faced each other once again, in impotent malevolence. The townie cousin whose name he couldn't think of would have had a word or an expression to describe the scene, but the man could not think what it might be. He strained his eyes along the crush pen for a discarded stick, not trusting his legs to follow. He tried to whistle. He cursed in baffled fury.

Where the hell was the bloody dog?

THE STUMP AND THE SAPLING

THE SPRING BEFORE HE HEARD about the child was mild, and the roots of the stump quickened blindly in the moist warm darkness, and burst the wall about the High Field into the laneway. Over the summer Paudie stemmed the rupture stone by stone as he could spare the time. Shoots sprouted in profusion from the ash-stool.

On a morning in winter he rose from where he lay before the fire in the kitchen, fanned the embers, and lit the rush wick from the flames. The earthen floor felt cold to his feet – colder than usual. His sleep had been uneasy, his thoughts and dreams full of what was happening in the bedroom. The sides of the settlebed, in the faint glow from the fire through the night, had seemed like a coffin's walls about him.

He fed tinder to the embers, fanned the bellows, and added peat sods, mounted the iron pot of soaking oatmeal onto the crook, and swung it over the heat. When the stirabout was cooked he placed the pot upon the hearthstone and knuckled the room door. He left the house before the old woman answered his summons. There was nothing unmanly in cooking a breakfast – he'd foraged for himself after his ma had died and before he'd taken a wife last year – but he would have felt ashamed in the presence of another who might talk about him doing woman's work.

Outside, day was breaking. The sky was as blue as a herring-man's cart, blue as Slieve Foy's peaked outline in the distance, the earth silver with frost. His breath about his face was the only cloud. He tended to the cow and calf, the fowl and the pigs, and the other morning chores. When he turned back to-wards the house there was a sharp white sliver atop the Cooley Mountains' rim. He squinted at the sun, crossed himself, and blessed the sight. A good sign, he thought. A healthy day, thank God. A fine hardy brittle winter day. A good day for a child to be born, as long as the house was warm.

Inside, the old woman who had never borne a live child of her own was walking from the room doorway to the table, her scraped-clean stirabout bowl in her hand. She turned at the rattle of the latch and looked at him across the half door, her sallow face a spider's web of wrinkles spun in grime, her lips unmoving in the hollow where her teeth had been. She dipped the tin into the water crock and filled a jug.

'Well?' he asked.

'She's alive.'

'Will she live?'

She looked at him in faint amusement as though he were a bright and innocent child.

'It's a long time now,' he mumbled, shamed suddenly by this intrusion into the world of women.

'I seen them go longer than this and live.'

Paudie nodded, one hand tugging at a strand of his grizzling beard. A midwife since boyhood to farmyard females, he knew that what his wife had already gone through was considerable.

He caught himself plucking, and stopped, and turned back to the yard.

After straining the half-bucketful of milk he'd stripped from the cow – all that she gave now, and she'd give less before she gave more – he breakfasted on lukewarm stirabout, then filled willow creels with peat sods, stacked them by the hearth, and built up the smoky fire. He left another creel by the room door. The house was still not warm. The turf harvest had been poor, and much of what he'd saved was damp, and burned with little heat. He brought a creel out to the fields and scavenged twigs and branches from the hedgerows – from as far as the outer ramparts of the fort itself. He respected the fairies but he didn't fear them. If there was need to, he'd bring firewood from the fort itself and face the consequences. But the less you had to do with fairies the better.

Returning through the High Field to the house, he paused, the creel no more than half-full on his shoulder. His gaze fell on the stump.

The sun was less than halfway up the sky when the notes of hoofbeats reached him on the frosty air. Above the hedge, along the sunken road, a bouncing felt hat warned of the bailiff's approach. Paudie's heart skipped a beat. In the excitement he'd forgotten. It had been a week since he'd paid his rent, though it seemed longer.

'Hi!' he shouted, and began to make his way to the hedge. 'Hi Phelim!'

The bailiff checked the cob. Paudie trotted up to him.

'Grand hardy morning,' the bailiff greeted.

'It is, thank God,' Paudie agreed. He added at once, 'You're on your way to Ellie-Owney's?' It wasn't so bad; the bailiff was alone. He wasn't going to road anyone – not today, at any rate.

The other nodded, his deeply socketed grey eyes watered by the cold in his silver-stubbled face. His thin lips tightened. He tugged the brim of his hat farther down before his eyes as he looked up at the man with the sun behind him. The cob threw a wall-eyed glare at the peasant and snatched a mouthful of grass, its teeth click-clacking on the bit.

Paudie hesitated. He twisted a strand of his beard around his finger, let it go.

'She's had a bad year of it,' he said eventually, staring over the horseman's head. The bailiff looked at him in silence. Paudie didn't meet his gaze. 'She had to sell the pig to pay the doctor,' he added. There was more to say: tuts and sighs and laments and all sorts of things that a man couldn't mention.

'So she toul me.'

Paudie hesitated. 'And the wee lassie died in the heel of it,' he managed to mention.

The bailiff's eyes and silence grew as frosty as the day.

'It's not aisy for her,' Paudie went on, a little hotly now, angered by life's mysterious injustices and obligations – Ellie-Owney was no relation – 'not aisy at all, with the man dead too, the youngest still in shitty rags, and the eldest just after taking his first half-year's pay home.'

'So she toul me,' the bailiff repeated, adding heavily: 'A week ago.'

'You might go aisy on her.'

'I did go aisy on her – a week ago.'

Paudie was desperate. Dambut-skin, she was a neighbour! 'She's three-ha'pence short.'

'So she toul me.'

'*Dhe*, are you an Irishman at all?' It was an explosive remark, and Paudie at once regretted it. The bailiff's eyes flashed in their sockets, surprised by such dangerous talk from this man. But he didn't even wipe the droplet of saliva from his cheek. He leaned forward in the saddle, one palm cupped on the pommel.

'Listen,' he said severely. 'I'm a man, that's what I am. And my wife's a woman. And my sons and my daughters are childer.' He took a deep breath, but his words sounded tired. 'Being Irish never put bread in our bellies. As far as Oul Bond's concerned, I could be a Dutchman, as long as I keep fetching in the rents. As far as the man in England is concerned, Oul Bond could be a Dutchman, as long as he keeps sending the rent money over.' He paused and raised his eyes a little, almost turned in the saddle, but didn't quite. 'I have to account for that three-ha'pence. If I let her go with it, where would it end? I'd be on the road myself.' He looked at Paudie's baffled face, and added on an angry note, 'I did all I could for her. I gave her a week.'

Aye, it was a cruel and un-Christian world a child was coming into!

'To hell with you,' Paudie growled, 'and the likes of you!' He realised that he too was not incapable of injustice, but his blood was up. 'Here's your bloody money.' He dug his hand into the pocket of his homespuns and gripped the small coins tightly. He felt like flinging them over the hedge. Four of them there were, two ha'pence and two farthings. Every wee bit helped, and now that there would be a child he could ill afford to part with any of it. But he couldn't let a woman and children be put on the road while he had money in his pocket that would save them. They were neighbours.

He dropped the coppers from the small height that he had over the bailiff in the sunken road, and the bailiff deftly caught them. He glanced at them, weighed them in his hand, then put them in a pocket of his waistcoat.

'Do you want a receipt?'

'No more nor I ever did!' Paudie said fiercely. 'You'll not forget.'

The bailiff looked up and sideways at him. He chuckled wryly. 'No, I wouldn't like to forget. What'll I tell her?' he added.

'Tell her nothing. Just say you'll get it off her next half-year. You can knock it off mine when you do.'

'Maybe I won't have to,' the bailiff said in a different, dangerous tone. 'What are you at there?'

A small finger of fear prodded Paudie in the belly. 'Just rooting and hoking,' he muttered.

'You're taking out the stump.'

Paudie said nothing. He had got four shillings for the timber, which no one begrudged him, but by removing the tree he had run the risk of increasing the rental value of his farm, and thereby his rent. It was a poor enough risk, and soon, please God, the Liberals would have their Land Act passed, which would give the farmers of Ireland secure tenure at a fair rent, and see to it that their own improvements would not be used as excuse to squeeze more out of them.

For now, however, this farm was better off – though it could be argued that there was now less shade for a beast in summer. Phelim wasn't the worst bailiff, and what Oul Bond didn't know wouldn't sicken anyone. Still, it was a risk. Three-ha'pence a half-year . . . Little enough, but enough to put them all on the road if he couldn't find it.

'You're taking out the stump,' the bailiff repeated.

'Aye.'

'Have you a horse?' The wintry smile seemed almost cruel.

'No,' Paudie replied, hotly again, of a sudden. 'But I've a sharp axe and a shovel – and a strong back, thank God.'

'Aye, and I'd say that if anyone'll do it it'll be yourself, you wee badger!' Phelim laughed. He touched the reins to the cob's neck and the animal trotted off.

Paudie returned to the stump. After he had felled the tree he had scorched the stump to kill it, so that the roots might rot. He had been sorry in a way to have destroyed the tree, and sourly pleased by the stump's defiance. A landmark it had been, and a beautiful tree, he'd always thought – though never, of course, remarked aloud. When he was a child it had seemed peopled with friendly shapes as it waved its topmost boughs at him – he had forgotten such foolish fancies until he was sweating over its corpse with axe and saw. As a young fellow coming home from hiring every half-year, he had welcomed its familiar outline on the horizon, and it had seemed to the child's eye that had never quite been blinded in his head that it too welcomed him. But it had been a huge old grandfather ash, its vast voracious roots an impoverishment to the little land he had. It had been time for it to go and past it. And now, when it was needed most, there was the stump. It would be difficult to get it broken up small enough to fit the hearth, but when done it would help keep life's breath in the child.

The springy roots resisted, gave grudging way before the axe. By midday he had encircled the stump. It was hard work, but he welcomed the effort. The surface of the ground was frozen hard, yet he was working in shirtsleeves. The sun was cheery if nothing else. It sparkled on the frost about him, and glittered on the cold deep blue of the sea in Dundalk Bay, miles distant. It was a good day for a child to be born.

Part of the attraction of the work was that it kept him from thinking about what was happening in the house. Since breakfast, and especially since that dig he'd got from Phelim, Paudie's guts hadn't felt quite right. But after the sun began its shallow decline he knew that he could put it off no longer. The neighbour woman from across the river, who called on most days now, hadn't shown so far, so Paudie had to take the wire basket and go himself to the pit in the garden and bring potatoes to the doorstep and wash them there. He filled the crock from the well at the Root of the Road, and called over the half door as he was leaving. From the muffled reply, he gathered that the child was still unborn, but still alive.

It surely couldn't take much longer. Not comparing the Christian to the brute beast, but what difference was there between his woman and his cow? Anxiety was gnawing now like rats at a bag of oats, so that he returned to the stump with a will. It took his mind off what was now beyond a doubt his fear. Once or twice, in the recent past, he had caught himself thinking pleasant thoughts about how nice it would be to have a son. Or even a daughter. To hear a child call him Da. Speculating on the sort of child his son might be, and the sort of man he would become.

But such vain thoughts were sinful, and now he felt guilty, and prayed to God to be forgiven. It was the woman he was thinking about now. It was the woman he was worried about. She'd be a terrible loss if anything went wrong. She was a grand woman. A good woman. He was very fond of her. He prayed to God to keep her.

A voice from the road broke into his thoughts. So intent on his work and his worries and his praying had he been that he hadn't heard the hoofbeats.

'Well?' Phelim called.

'Well yourself.' Paudie put on his coat. Already the sweat was chilling him. He walked to the hedge. The cob snorted smokily through pinkish nostrils, tossed its ugly hammerhead to get more rein, and nibbled the cold dead grass across the bit. 'How did you leave Ellie-Owney?' Paudie asked.

'For another half-year, that's how. How are you getting on?'

'Not so bad.'

'A horse would be a mighty help,' Phelim said, with that mocking smile hiding in his sunken eyes.

'I'm sure he would,' Paudie agreed, 'if I had a horse.' He knew that any way he chose to ask he could borrow the cob for as long as it took to haul the stump out of the ground. It would save half a day. But he was a stubborn man and he had his pride, and in any event the work was welcome. 'But sure in a few years' time,' he went on rather loftily, 'if Gladstone has his way, I'll have my land, and a few years after that, with the help o' God, I'll have my horse – when maybe the likes of you won't.'

The bailiff laughed, not at all put out. 'When that day dawns,' he said drily, 'I'll maybe sell you this fellow. But I'll tell you one thing,' he went on, leaning forward on the pommel. 'It won't matter a damn who's in, Gladstone or Disraeli. Aye, or Parnell himself. You'll still be a poor man, and so will I. And don't be surprised if your son and your grandson are still paying rent on your poor wee acres long after you're dust. What King Billy said to the Boyne boatman was the truth: It won't matter who wins the battle, my man, you'll still be rowing this boat.'

Paudie laughed in turn, no more put out than the other. He rather suspected that what the bailiff said was true. King Billy had been a Dutchman, but Phelim spoke sense, and there were wicked flints of wisdom in the gravel of his words to lame the unwary who would press him too closely. But still, what sort of a world would Paudie be making for his son and his grandson, and the sons who came after, if he was to believe in such sense as that?

The bailiff took out his pipe and tobacco. Paudie declined the offer of a fill, but in a mannerly fashion. He waited until the other had the pipe lit to his satisfaction, though he was anxious to return to his work.

'I passed oul Mary-Ellen McCabe's house,' Phelim said suddenly. 'She wasn't about. Is it your woman's time?'

Paudie nodded.

'God send you a strong son. G'along there.'

The bailiff tongue-clicked round his pipe stem, and the cob set off.

The sun had gone far down when Paudie heard the hoofbeats from the road again. He had worked savagely as the evening had advanced, driving himself to limits that left no time to think further ahead than where he should plant the next swing of the axe's heavy blade, the next swing of the shovel; no time to give to the slack unmanly feeling in his belly, to the brassy taste of his tongue.

It was too long. All day and the previous night she'd been under it, and God knew how much of the previous day, before he'd found her on the hearthstone. God spare her, he prayed. He was resigned to the death of the child, for many a child died. They could have more, as long as He spared Briege.

He paused and waited for the call from the road, remembering the last sound he'd heard, an hour or more ago: a short reedy scream from the house. Only the one, distant as the dawn, muffled immediately. At first he had taken pride in the way she could control herself so well, but then a sinister significance had struck him, and stayed weighing on his shoulders like a raven. Exhaustion hit him now. He had to take a deep breath to answer the bailiff's call. He heard the rustle of the winter-hardened hedge as a foot stepped out of a stirrup onto it, and then the shadow of Phelim's broad body filled the dark hollow in which he was crouched.

'By *Dhe* you could use a horse right enough.'

'I'll get one of my own then.'

'Aren't you the thick headstrong wee man,' the bailiff said in a quiet voice. But he broke off as he studied the scene in the fading light and swore again, more sharply. '*Dhe*, you're an awful man!'

A circular trench over ten feet in diameter opened at his feet.

From this trench Paudie had undermined the stump, under-pinning it with such lengths of old timber and tree branches as he'd been able to lay hands on. As he'd worked his way across, he'd levered the stump up on one side, canting it at an angle. Now he was crouched under the huge mass, hacking at the remaining roots as best he could in the confined space. It was no inconsiderable risk he was taking: if the props should slip, he would be crushed or smothered.

'An awful man,' the bailiff repeated. 'Come out of there this minute! Is it that you want to make your child an orphan, and your wife a widow?' Paudie didn't waste breath saying that his child must be dead by now, and his woman maybe too.

'Come out!' Phelim said urgently. 'Don't be a fool all your life.'

'Come out!' he shouted, as though he'd heard the deep intake of breath. 'I'm getting the cob.'

There was a sudden dry crackling noise. The props tumbled into the excavation. The stump teetered like a run-down scourging top. Phelim crossed himself and muttered some-thing. Slowly the mass began to move, away from him. He heard the small man grunt. Then the stump rolled onto its side, with one last creaking protest from the remaining roots.

'*A Dhia!*' the bailiff breathed. 'Here.' He stretched out his hand. Paudie took it. Phelim heaved him out. 'Holy God! Do you know, you're the tightest wee man I ever seen in my life. The tightest wee man I ever seen.' He laughed, gleefully. In the near-darkness, Paudie was a darker shape, coated from head to foot in damp earth and weathered carbon. Phelim shook his head in wonder, staring at the stump. 'Yon thing's half a ton if it's an ounce.'

Paudie didn't answer. His mind was with his woman.

'Tell you what I'll do,' the bailiff said with a thoughtful air. 'Next time I'm passing, I'll bring a blasting stick with me. I'll drill that thing and split it for you. You'd never do it with wedges.'

Paudie nodded, hardly hearing. Now that he was going home, the taste of poison metal in his mouth was stronger than ever.

'What took you back?' His own voice sounded strange.

'Ach, I had another wee bit of business back the road a bit,' Phelim said vaguely. 'I just rode over to see how you were getting on. I thought you might have need of a horse.'

'I'll have one of my own some day.'

'I'd say you will too.'

The evening was chilling Paudie through the sweat and the earth that clung to him. He shivered. They walked together towards the house.

'An odd touch o' spring to that day, wasn't there?' Phelim observed. 'For all the frost.'

Paudie nodded. He thought that in all his life he had never been really afraid of anything until now.

The bailiff didn't speak again until they were entering the yard, and when he did so it was in a quiet voice.

'How's the woman?'

'We'll see.'

They smelled boiled potatoes across the half door. A faint glow from the fire and the rush wick was in the kitchen. The old woman was a flickering ghost beside the hearth, her bare feet in the ashes, her clay pipe in the hollow of her face.

'Well?' Paudie asked gruffly.

'She'll be grand.'

'Thank God!' He wished suddenly that he could sit down. 'Thank God!' The tremor in his voice shamed him. But then another thought occurred. 'And the child?'

The old woman's smile was unmistakable, for all the gloom and gummy darkness.

'A grand wee *gasún*, God bless him. A tight wee man child, the image of his father!'

Phelim slapped him on the back and laughed loudly, as though the triumph were the man's.

'Good man yourself!' He grabbed Paudie's hand and shook it, and closed it firmly on something small and hard. 'That's for the child,' he whispered. 'For when you're christening him.'

Paudie felt one of the small coins he'd half-thrown in the bailiff's face that morning.

'Thanks, Phelim,' he muttered, ashamed of his temper earlier. 'Thanks and good luck.'

'You're welcome. Goodbye and good luck.'

There was silence in the kitchen. Paudie's mouth was dry again, but it was the dryness of excitement. The empty feeling in his belly had turned to raging hunger, but he had no thought of grub. He wanted to ask more about his woman, but would have been shamed by the unmanliness of such a query.

But the old woman might have heard him thinking. 'Briege is sleeping now,' she said. 'I left all she'll need inside with her. The fire's stacked. I'll cross the plank by Hughes's on my way home and tell Molly. She'll drop over in the morning. The settlebed's made up for you.'

She came close – 'Here!' – and thrust something at him. It was the chamberpot. 'Bury that,' she whispered urgently, 'this very night!'

Paudie looked into it in confusion. There was a dark-coloured ropy bloody mess whose like he had often seen after calvings and farrowings. He felt himself flush, and was glad of the gloom.

The old woman's bony fingers were like talons on his el-bow. '*Éist* to me now. Take that to the fort, and bury it under a fairy tree. A rowan, or a thorn. They might think he was born dead. But still, whatever you do, never leave that child without the tongs over the cradle, for they can't cross iron. And they'd take him, so they would, if they got the chance. He's a fine *gasún*. There's more nor the Shining Ones would steal him.'

After she left, Paudie crept to the door of the room. He hesitated, feeling oddly shy. Holding the rush wick low and behind him, he opened the door. The faint familiar smell of damp walls and slopped night-water and ancient man- and woman-sweat filled his nostrils. Peat sods glowed on the small hearth. He could hear his woman breathing, and another, lighter, living sound.

'Briege?' he whispered.

There was a pause. 'What?'

He hesitated. 'Are you all right?'

'Aye.'

When he spoke again his voice was shaky, but he didn't feel unmanned. 'You're a good woman, Briege. I'm thanking God for sparing you.'

She sighed, and said in a voice made hoarse, he supposed, by weariness and her recent hardship, 'You're a good man, Paudie.'

He withdrew, then opened the door again, and raised the greasy light.

The child was in the world, a tiny mop of black hair at his mother's breast, as great a miracle as the rising of the sun.

'And the child?' he whispered.

'He's all right. I'm tired, Paudie. Let me rest.'

'Goodnight, Briege. God take care of you – the two of you.'

He washed himself, then milked the cow and tended the stock again, shaking an extra armful of bedding beneath each beast. It was a hard old world and always would be, but he felt like laughing as he patted the hairy hides. Back in the kitchen he soaked oatmeal for the breakfast, built up the fire, and stretched his feet to the heat. He was jaded. He spotted the chamberpot – no rest for him yet. He remembered the old woman's warnings. There would be some truth in her words, more than there was in what the new priest was saying, about fairies being a lot of pagan nonsense and *piseogs*. They were God's Fallen Angels, after all, whom God had spared from falling all the way. It was well to keep great with them. But Paudie's own belief was that the less you had to do with them the more they'd leave you alone. He wouldn't go near the fort. By the time they found out about him, the child might be too big for them to bother with. Very young children, fairies were mostly interested in. Very young children, and dying women.

But what was he to do about it? About the – whatever it was you'd properly call it? He gazed at the images shimmering in the coals, tugging at his beard for many pleasant minutes, and decided.

He'd dig a hole in that awkward wee corner of the garden and empty the chamberpot there. Being honest with himself, he didn't fancy going near the fort after dark.

Later, in the settlebed, he lay awake for all his weariness, murmuring prayers of thanks, and thinking. His son had been born today; his woman had been spared. Today was a day he would never forget, one that the world should remember.

There was an ash sapling growing hard against the gable of the barn, sprung from a seed, no doubt, of the old giant he'd slaughtered. It would knock the wall in time if it wasn't shifted out of there. He'd dig it up and save the roots, transplant it over the – thing he'd just buried. It hadn't been an animal's cleanings, that could be thrown where dogs might get it, underneath a sod or in the dunghill. A grave, you'd have to call what he'd just made. He'd transplant the sapling to the grave. The tree had no business being where it was, but in that wee corner of the garden ...

It was a landmark to outlive them all that God would raise to mark the day.

COWARD!

'COWARD!' HE CALLED ME on the day we met, and he must have been correct. It's not a brave man who hides behind drawn curtains, living off a woman's earnings, sending her or a boy on crutches, his own son, to ask 'Who's there?' when doorbells ring, and crouches in the shadows, fingers hooked on triggers, thumb against the safety. The brand-new shotgun's always loaded – dangerous I know, with a child in the house, but I'm afraid to put myself at any disadvantage, and I keep it on a high shelf when I leave it out of hand, or beneath the bed I share again with Eleanor, when I try to sleep. There isn't a hope that they'd believe me – I know that. And I know they'd have no mercy, and I'm afraid they'd take their time. Civilisation is the thinnest of veneers on the most urbane of us, I realise that now. None of us is excepted – certainly not me. The papers tell us every day of their atrocities. But I don't judge them. Not their consciences. Not I. Not now.

Sometimes the mere touching of a gun appals me still. He was right in so much, even as a child. Perhaps I've been a coward all my life.

I didn't even know the meaning of the word when first I heard it. I reacted to his jeering, taunting tone. I suppose it was my first fight. We had more in the years that followed. Three, four – maybe ten or twelve. I can only recall the first and last at school. And that other one, of course; that final one, years later.

The first remains a memory of a blow to my nose; the blinding pain of it; then the fear; finally the prickly, agonising effort to sneeze through the sobs when it was over. And always that triumphant ringing 'Coward!' The last was different – the last at school I mean, not the one last month. The fear had come first, as it always did by then. But towards the end I landed a wild swing right in his face. The blood exploded from his nose and he fell down dazed.

I let him up of course. I was terrified that I had seriously hurt him, and I lacked the fighter's instinct. But the look of murder in his eyes and the frenzied stretch of his lips over set teeth gave desperation to my terror, and we were both spattered by blood, and slugging it toe to toe, when the master strode between us and held us at arm's length by an ear apiece, apart.

We were taken separately out the back and punished, and stood in opposite corners of the classroom until home time. Then the master sent him on ahead and warned him not to tarry, and spoke quietly of his disappointment with me.

At a safe distance from the school he was waiting.

I almost cried at the sight of him, but his smile was not quite hostile and he made no move. When I came close he spoke.

'How many did he give you?'

'Six.'

'Bastard gave me ten! Did you say I started it?'

I was going to tell a lie but something stopped me. 'Aye.'

'I said you did.' He laughed. 'Who did start it?'

I considered. 'I think you did.'

'Did I?' He laughed again and I smiled. We walked together to the crossroads.

That would have been the spring before the eleven-plus results came out, and in September we went our separate ways, he to the newly opened Intermediate in Crossmaglen, I to a grammar school in Newry. We were all surprised he'd failed. The master, for all that he'd never hidden his dislike for Brian, made no secret of his dismay either. But Brian didn't seem to mind. If he didn't know exactly what he wanted then, he had the air of one with every confidence of finding out. We saw little of each other afterwards, except at Mass on Sundays, or at marts with our fathers, but he always had that wolfish smile and a friendly word for me.

We had our first drink together the evening A-level results came out. I was with some of my grammar-school pals celebrating, experimenting gingerly with cider, when he approached out of the pool room, stout froth browning his fuzzy moustache. He asked if there was any crack, and I told him about the exams. He whispered that he had a girl in trouble, eyeing me wickedly, and my virginity became an exasperation and embarrassment. Perhaps I coloured, for he clapped me on the back and laughed.

'Just codding Tony! Don't think I'd do a silly thing like that?'

I introduced him to the others with a mixture of feelings: condescension towards his labourer's overalls, an irritated, reluctant admiration for his full-grown rugged figure, most of all with apprehension. I let them see me smile at his uncouthness and broad south Armagh accent. Two of them were talking overloudly, full of shit and shandy, about *The Seven Pillars of Wisdom* and whether Lawrence had been homosexual. Brian interrupted.

'Did any o' yous ever read a story called *Dorian Gray*? Powerful book, boy! Powerful book.'

We sniggered in tipsy intellectual superiority, and his lupine grin was faint as he looked at each of us in turn – in puzzlement, we thought. He went back to the pool room, but not before he bought a pint of Stag for me. I felt a little mean, but giggled with the others when he'd gone.

University, and later work, kept me in London for over fifteen years, and it was only after the split with Eleanor occurred and I returned home to south Armagh to take stock of my life that I got to know him again. I'd intended to stay for no more than a week or two, emotionally recuperating in the quiet of Slieve Gullion's shadow and the imagined tranquillity of Carlingford's reflection of the mountains' stillness. But then I met another architect in Newry, just gone into business for himself and willing to consider taking on a partner. The building trade was in recession, but Frank had built up contacts and goodwill, and, as he said breezily, no problem lasts forever. He gave me some work, and as I had a little bit of money put by I decided to stay a while – until, perhaps, Eleanor was starting to have regrets.

When Frank and I were drinking in Dundalk one night, he came to our table, strong teeth topped by a thick Zapata moustache, and stretched out a big hard hand in welcome. I'd seen him once or twice around the town, but at a distance, and hadn't approached him. Now I feigned a struggle to put a name to him, but he was not put out, and laughed in triumph when I said eventually, 'Brian McStravick!'

'Ahoy you boy you, Tony.'

But through all the smiling friendliness there was a calculation to his grin that I could not remember being there before. It reminded me of a fox's rather than a wolf's now.

The scarred knuckles and ingrained grime of his hands made the information that he was mechanicking no surprise, and as we were running short of things to say, I asked if he knew where I might pick up a boat, second-hand. I'd been out with Frank in his the previous weekend, and rather fancied the thought of having my own.

Brian considered. 'I might. Do you know Xavier Boale?' he asked Frank. Frank shook his head. 'He has one he might sell.' Brian turned his attention back to me. 'A twelve-foot fibreglass with a vee hull and a Yamaha outboard, going with her or separate. I'll have a word and get back to you. What sort o' shillings would she need to be coming into you at?'

'I'd need to see it first.' I didn't have a clue as to what such a boat might be worth, but Brian was waiting expectantly, and there was an amused sort of smirk about Frank's face as he looked on. 'I wouldn't want to go over – oh, half – forty per cent the value of a new one.'

Brian chuckled. 'Ach we'll get you fixed up for far less than that. Are you on the phone?'

He rang Frank's office the next day.

'He's selling all right, but not as cheap as I thought, and I'd say he'll hold out for his price.'

I remembered his foxy look and guessed that he'd be keeping a fat commission for himself, so expressed no more than casual interest.

'Ach there's no push, Tony. Xavier doesn't give a shit whether she sells or not. You can have a look and see what you think. If you're doing nothing Sunday I'll see you in Carlingford, and you can take her out and try her.'

I met him in the Rapparee's Rest at one o'clock and we had two pints each and went down to the pier. He mentioned a price as we walked, and I whistled, still without much notion as to the value of such a boat.

'As I said, she isn't cheap, but sure we'll have a day out in her anyway.' He laughed. He filled the tank and set the fuel drum down in the bilge where a coiled-up rope was nestling with a pair of skis. There were two oars and a short sharp gaff with a T-handle – the sort they used to hook into pigs' cheeks to hold them for the sledgehammer in the days of farmyard slaughtering. For landing salmon, I supposed; perhaps a makeshift boat-hook.

'Did you ever try this?' Brian gestured towards the skis.

'Once or twice. I was never very good.'

'I'll teach you then. I'm not bad at it myself. It's great crack.' Again the laugh.

The engine was a fifty-five-horsepower unit, and hard to start. It seemed strong, but thinking ahead to the bargaining I'd have to do if I was buying, I criticised it. Brian nodded.

'Ach she's seen better days, I suppose. But the boat's near new and tell you what: if you do decide to buy I'll work something out with Boale and do the motor up for you in the price. New rings, pistons and barrels if she needs them, a water pump and new reeds. I'll see you're not done wrong. They're good engines, there's little goes wrong with them. Just keep the mix right and they'll run for years.'

I felt quietly smug and stayed noncommittal.

We messed around for an hour or so. He gave me the controls.

'Plenty o' welly! Plenty o' welly!' – laughing – 'she'll take it. Just keep her this side of the lough – don't want to be stepping on her majesty's tits!'

He tossed the towrope over the stern, slipped into the water, and put on the skis. The boat was noticeably slower with the extra drag, and I had to keep the throttle against the stop to haul him out of the water. When he was on the surface, though, it was easier. I towed him to the Greenore Bar and swung in a wide arc towards Greencastle, and when the breeze brought his words to me, did as he instructed and turned back towards the southern shore.

We went up past Omeath. I distinguished words over the noise of the engine and the boyish yelps and laughter, and complied and turned again. I went out quite far towards Warrenpoint, enjoying the mastery of the skipping craft, and with my preoccupied excitement and the salty breeze in my face could no longer hear him clearly. But suddenly I became aware that he was shouting.

I looked back and he took one hand off the towrope and jerked rapidly towards Omeath. There was a big grey inflatable moving towards us from the north side. I turned as directed but he was still shouting, and then the boat began to jerk. When I turned again to look, he was hauling himself hand over hand along the umbilical rope. The inflatable was very close now, and between us and the southern shore. I could see a taut look on Brian's face and realised that something was wrong.

I knew that what he was going to do was dangerous, and throttled back as he went to throw himself into the boat. But he swore and told me to 'go like fuck!' I'd never seen fear in his face before. The other craft was abreast of us, no more than a few boat-widths away. I could see men in camouflage uniform: a British naval patrol.

As soon as Brian got into the boat it picked up speed. He pushed me aside and grabbed the controls. The big inflatable closed in on us. One of the marines was swinging a rope with something heavy on the end. A grappling hook.

'Take this.' Brian grabbed an oar and raised its end to me, steering away from them, back towards the middle of the lough, ducking and weaving. 'Quick, fuck you. Take it! Keep them off. They'll lift you too if they get aboard.'

A confused man, a frightened man, will generally do as he's told. That's all I can say. I obeyed. A lucky swing deflected the flying hook. Brian's skilful handling evaded their next few attempts. But inevitably they caught the gunwhale amidships, and we slewed as they came alongside.

'Hit them, hit them!' Brian was shouting. 'No you silly cunt, poke them – hard.' I'd been trying to use the oar as an unwieldy club. Terrified, mystified, blindly obedient, I thrust half-heartedly at the soldier nearest me, the one straining on the rope. He was young, with an eager, hard look, a confident, predatory smile stretching his lips. Another in their bows was targeting Brian, ready to leap. A third was at the wheel. There was a fourth soldier, hanging back, looking very young and scared, green-faced and slack-jawed. My oar glanced off the shoulder of my adversary. The boat rocked a little. The soldier snarled.

Suddenly there was the dull sound of a blow and an instant later someone screamed. I glanced forward. The second soldier was falling back, his hands pawing at his face, blood pumping from a gash that had been opened from his forehead to his jaw. His cheek was a flittered rag. His eye may have been in the spilling mess.

The snarling soldier drew back, his snarl petrifying. The rope slackened. The boat yawed crazily as Brian threw himself past me, knocking me sprawling in the bilge. The short gaff was in his hand. Its hook was red. I got a glimpse of the green-faced child in camouflage splashing vomit.

'The throttle! Quick, the wheel!'

I scrambled to obey. He hooked the handle of the gaff into the grappling iron and flicked it over the side. I reached the controls and opened up, heading for the Omeath side.

'Not too close,' Brian said eventually. His voice was calm.

The marines were gone. I steered out a little. I was shaking. My guts were slack and my legs were weak. I felt light-headed and sick, as though I might be about to faint. We didn't speak another word until we got to Carlingford. Brian stowed away the oars and rope, washed the gore off the gaff, and tied up. I pissed on the pier while he dressed. We set off up the village.

'What the hell was that about?' Back on dry land, it felt safe to express self-righteous anger.

He didn't reply at once. 'Tell you in the Rapparee.'

We took a quiet corner. 'A pint?' he asked.

'A brandy.'

We sipped in silence for a few thoughtful moments. Then he laughed, softly and without mirth. Ruefully. 'I'm sorry, Tony. I'm sorry I got you involved.'

'Involved in what, damn you?' I was staring straight ahead, fighting tears of fright and fear, my anger inadequate, knowing only too well what.

'I was the election agent for the Sinn Féin candidate in the last elections here.'

'You mean the IRA candidate?'

'The Sinn Féin candidate.'

'What's the difference, pray?'

He chuckled dryly, seemed as though he might reply, but didn't. 'Good luck!' he said instead, and raised his pint glass to his lips. I tried to follow suit, but my hands were trembling so hard I knew I'd spill the brandy if I did so. The more I tried to still the trembling the worse it got, until my muscles became physically sore. I could feel the heavy teardrops weighing down my eyelashes.

Brian leaned forward and grasped my wrist. The glass stilled. He spoke sincerely. 'Hey Tony, don't feel bad. You did all right. It's okay. I know how you feel. First action ever I was in, I pissed myself – literally.'

I burst into laughter: of bitterness, self-mockery – gallows laughter. Whether Brian mistook it for the real thing or chose to pretend to do so – or felt the same way himself, perhaps – he chorused with his customary loudness, and we chortled and howled until the barman stared.

Brian took a huge gulp from his stout and motioned. 'Knock that back and have another. They're all on me.'

The trembling had gone from my hand. I drank two brandies within ten minutes, then switched to pints of ale. After the third of these it was easy to persuade me.

'Indeed and you're not!' I'd just told him I was driving, in response to an exhortation to have another. 'It's not every day you miss out on Palace Barracks as close as we did today. A mate o' mine has a house here. We'll stay and celebrate. I've got a key.'

'Will he mind?'

'He's not around. He's in the States, selling Aran sweaters and Celtic crosses from the Kesh to fat-arsed Yanks with loads of money.'

I sensed darkly where the revenue would be going, but felt like getting drunk too much to worry about whose hospitality I'd be accepting. But at some stage of my inebriation I felt I had to say something.

'I couldn't kill a man to save my life, you know that? The thought of even hitting a man appals me.' I was sorry then for saying that, for I was afraid that he might think it was simply an excuse for my poor showing against the soldiers.

'You might be surprised,' he said, after a moment.

Still worried that he might think I was merely making ex-cuses, I held my tongue. But a few mouthfuls later I had to ask, 'Are you in Sinn Féin or the IRA?'

He took so long to answer that I was beginning to think, a little gratefully, that he wouldn't. But he said, 'When all the fences are down you have to stand somewhere on your own two feet.'

It made no sense, sounded like an excuse of his own for something worse. But I felt it might be a lame rebuke, so I emphasised, 'I couldn't kill a fellow human being to save my own life, far less over a few troublesome counties. It just isn't worth it!'

His silence seemed thoughtful more than tactful, and I believed I'd made my point.

It was after hours when we left, and the two of us were drunk. As we staggered up the street he asked if I was married and I told him I wasn't. He'd asked me before and I'd told him the same. I knew how differently such an arrangement as I'd had with Eleanor might be viewed here, and besides, I just didn't feel like talking about her and Jason to a stranger. I was missing them with a far sharper pain than I still felt regularly, regretting the break-up. But I put it down to the fright I'd had that afternoon and the need for comfort, and downright drunken sentimentality.

The electricity had been disconnected in the house, but Brian found candles and put a kettle on the gas ring and made coffee, lacing it liberally with the brandy that he'd bought. He sat beside me on the couch and clapped a friendly hand on my knee.

'Well begod that was some crack, right?' He laughed. I agreed. He laughed again, very loudly. 'So you're not married?' he asked after a pause.

'No.'

'Ever close?'

I'd had two live-in relationships before the one with Eleanor but had never seriously considered formalising any of them, except briefly after Jason had been conceived. I almost told him, but for some reason said no.

'Me neither,' he said contentedly, and there was silence. His hand was on my knee still. I moved under some pretext and dislodged it. The silence became strained.

He laughed softly, and threw his arm across my shoulder. 'Some day, huh?'

I leaned forward deliberately and turned to face him so that his hand dropped off, down my back, onto the couch. 'Yeah,' I answered warily.

The silence was definitely awkward this time. Brian laughed quietly again. 'Women – ach! I never could get on with women.'

I was opening my mouth to tell him then, aware of what was happening, but he beat me to it.

'I used to think that there was something wrong with me. Y'know? Now I know I'm just different. No better and no worse. Like lots of men. Like you, Tony – huh?'

I took a deep breath. 'No Brian, not like me.'

His hand was on my leg again, a little higher. I removed it. He replaced it. I tried to lift it off again, but he tightened his grip. There was a lot of power in that hand.

'I've got a son in England. I've slept with lots of women. I'm straight. AC only. I've never had any homosexual inclinations.'

'Gay,' he murmured. 'Don't use that other ugly word.'

His hand crept higher. I wrenched it away.

'Look Brian, forget it. There's no way – that's the end of it. Okay?'

He hesitated. 'Just because you've had a woman – women – even a child: that doesn't change it. You're gay, Tony, I can tell. You just don't know it yet, maybe.' His voice was hypnotic. 'Did you know that Wilde was twenty-six – ?'

'Look, lay off, man! You're out of order. There's no way – ' I broke off and stood swaying. The room was going round.

My stomach churned. 'I'm going home.'

'No you're not!' His tone changed. 'You're staying here with me. You're scared now, but you'll thank me in the morning.'

'No!' I was trying to sober up, cursing my greed of the evening, becoming seriously alarmed. The situation had gone rapidly from an embarrassment to one fraught with real menace. He was bigger and much stronger than I, and didn't appear to be nearly as drunk – probably just drunk enough to be most dangerous. The casually brutal way in which he'd disposed of the unfortunate soldier that afternoon was vivid in my mind.

'Look Brian, forget it, please. There's been a misunderstanding, and I think it would be best if I went home.'

He moved between me and the door and blocked me, reaching out. I slapped his hand aside. His voice when he spoke sounded husky and excited.

'So you like it rough, do you? Well so do I – the rougher the better. C'm'ere, baby.'

That endearment revolted me. Something snapped inside. I lunged at him and screamed.

'Fuck off you pervert! Get your filthy paws off me, you dirty queer!'

'Don't use that word!' he roared. And then we closed.

All my liberal notions and tolerance were swept away by the revulsion that erupted like pus from a shiny scab, burst by the thought of the loathsome obscenity. I punched and kicked and butted, snapped at his face in a clinch once, poked fingers at his eyes, desperate to get away.

It was by far the worst fight I'd ever been in through school and undergraduate wild days, and it reminded me of my first: the stinging pain of my nose and lips, but more so the terror and its strange novelty. We knocked a candle over and it went out, and we flailed away in the half-darkness. He took most of my blows on his forearms and thighs, but my fists and knees and feet jarred solidly more than once, and I was beginning to think that I might be getting the upper hand when a foot wrapped round my ankle and I sprawled. Next thing he was heavy on top of me, with one arm twisted up my back, and I was helpless.

A sob of fear bubbled from my guts, choking as it rose, escaped as a childish bawl. My stomach heaved and I disgorged upon the floor. He let me retch and cry for quite some time, then his grip loosened and his weight eased. Eventually I realised that I could get up, but even when he rose and righted and relit the candle, I was too cowed to do anything but roll upon my side to eye him, away from the pool of vomit.

He was staring at something behind me, smiling faintly, and if his face showed anything it was a bleak sort of wistfulness.

'Come on,' he said gently then, reaching out a hand. I cringed. 'Get up, Tony, I won't hurt you. I swear to God. I couldn't rape anyone, far less a friend. But you needed taking down a peg.'

A tiny flame flickered in the embers of my anger. 'What do you mean?'

'How long is it since you said you couldn't kill a man? Couldn't even hit a man? To save your life? Three hours?'

My anger was snuffed out in its ashes. He had to say no more and must have known that, but he emphasised his point with sudden self-righteous anger of his own: 'Never, ever, the longest day you live, judge anybody else's conscience! Judge their deeds if you have to, or if you think you have the right. But there's nothing the worst man on earth can do that *you* couldn't do too, given the right circumstances.' He paused for breath and licked his lips. 'If you have to judge a conscience judge your own, and leave the rest to God.'

I saw the blood upon his nose, his swollen mouth, his eyes already puffed, and realised my own condition; that he had landed only a few stinging slaps and slackened fists. I looked at his muscular physique, the size of his hands, and knew then that he could have killed me had he wished, as I would have killed him if I could.

It took only a little time for the lesson he had taught to hammer home – I honestly am a pretty open-minded individual – most of the time. I felt like thanking him then, for teaching me, for sparing me, for saving me that day, yet couldn't find the words. But when I reached my cup out towards the proffered bottle and he laughed, I knew he knew.

We got drunk again, but differently. We talked the sun up, mostly about the Troubles, but in a detached, almost academic way. It would have been easy for an eavesdropper to fail to realise that Brian had a personal involvement in them, so objective and reasonable were his arguments, so genuine did his expressed regret for the victims on every side appear. The only giveaway was the repeated remark: 'When all the fences are down, you have to stand somewhere on your own two feet.'

Towards the end we both got more light-hearted, and laughed and joked about the fights we'd had at school and others afterwards; and about women, for he'd had his share of those as well. As we wobbled to our separate rooms he promised to take me out again on Thursday, his half-day,

'– in Xavier's *big* boat. Man she'll shift! The Brits'll never expect me to be out midweek, and even if the bastards do chase us, they'll never catch us in that. I know two lassies might come with us. They're like me, but one's a switch-hitter. I think you'd like her. She's into art and that, and she's a good-looker. We'll bring some wine and grub – make a day of it. Are you on?'

I agreed.

We both were very ill next day, but his bruised face was smiling. 'Rough night last night! Quare day, what? You still on for Thursday?'

I nodded, though I was having second thoughts already. I realised that there was a lot of depth to Brian – I even sensed a certain goodness – and I realised that I liked him; that despite his unorthodox sexual preferences and our disparate views on the Troubles, we could be friends. But if he was in the IRA I was afraid of getting into trouble by association. I determined to sever my contact with him, but gradually and decently, and decided that I could afford to go with him on Thursday. To be honest I was intrigued by the girls of whom he'd spoken. It had been months since I'd had any sex.

But as our appointment drew nearer my reservations mounted. I told Frank about the episode on the lough, and he confirmed that it could spell very serious trouble for me if, or rather when, the British Army should learn my identity. He said that he had a cousin in the RUC, and that if I liked he could arrange a meeting with this man, explain the circumstances to him, and see if the message could be trickled through to the British that I had been an unwitting and unwilling accomplice to the skirmish on the lough. But he didn't need to tell me that if I were seen again with Brian it would be difficult to make that seem credible. I sought for an excuse to stay away that Thursday, but kept putting off a call to Brian.

In the end I had a valid reason not to go with him. A telegram, more than twelve hours old, arrived that very morning, telling me to phone Eleanor at once.

Jason had been struck by a car the evening before, coming home from school. Frank drove me to the airport.

My son had sustained two broken legs and severe concussion, but was in no danger. I felt enormous relief, and a sense of belonging, being with him and Eleanor; a sense of being needed; and a sense of joy. It was like coming home, as my return to south Armagh had not been. I stayed with Eleanor that night. Next day Frank phoned.

Brian and two companions had been arrested by a British naval patrol on Carlingford Lough that Thursday afternoon. His boat had broken down. There was talk of sabotage, and tip-offs; of a coward's vengeance. Friends of his were looking for me.

Last night there was a drill bit in my dreams, grinding through my kneecaps. I woke up screaming. Eleanor's going to bits along with me. She says she can't take much more. Jason looks hunted and guilty. He's become very much withdrawn. His recovery seems slow. He doesn't seem to like me any more.

Eleanor wants me to ask for police protection. What a joke. She's English, of course, and doesn't understand. Apart from anything else, the police have more pressing things to do than give protection to a coward. For I suppose that's what I am. I wasn't such a fool as to have actually run away from trouble, but if I hadn't been a coward I'd have gone back to explain. It's too late to do that now. Even Brian must believe by this time – though I'm convinced he didn't at the start – that I set him up.

It's hard to see any way out. The latest word from Frank is that that soldier lost an eye, and that one of the charges the Crown is likely to bring against Brian, the one with the best chance of being proved, is of malicious wounding. If I approach the authorities, I'm going to be pressed into giving evidence against him. If I do, I'm a dead man. If I don't, I'll most likely be charged with being an accessory, and remanded in custody, perhaps with republican prisoners. Still a dead man.

So what do I do? It's impossible to hide. They're the most successful terrorists in the world. They can hit barracked soldiers in Germany, cavalry patrols in the heart of London, for God's sake. I'll be no more than an hour's work some slack evening. Or a whole night's awful fun. They must know about Eleanor by now, know where she works, must follow her home some time. Eventually the truant officer is going to come looking for Jason, and if he goes back to school, and they take him hostage on the way, of what use is my shotgun to me then?

Eleanor threatens to throw me out – or turn me in. Sometimes I almost hope she will. As Brian was so fond of saying, when all the fences are down, a man has to stand somewhere on his own two feet. Sometimes I'm afraid my fear will drive me mad – that it's doing so already. Sometimes I feel that the only greasy grip I've left on sanity are the words Frank said one time, that no problem lasts forever. I know he's right. But I hope I don't solve this one with the shotgun's barrels in my corpse's mouth. That would be a coward's way.

A LAND FIT FOR HEROES

AFTER VON KLUCK INVADED, Peter Gibson's father went off, one of the first, to teach the Hun a lesson, to save gallant – though Catholic – little Belgium, and, finally, to win the war that would end all wars. Peter was there, in Belfast, to cheer his father and the other brave soldiers of the Ulster regiments along the streets when they were welcomed home as heroes, in the spring of 1919. Brass bands played 'God Save the King', and 'Rule Britannia', and the other songs: 'The Sash', 'The Walls of Derry', 'Lillibulero'. There was the riotous reek of whiskey and porter and tobacco from the wild-eyed dark-mouthed yelling men, tears in the eyes of the women and girls, the rough brush of tweed against Peter's cheeks in the throng. Later they – his mother, his younger brother and sister, and Peter – took the Great Northern Railway home to County Monaghan; his father followed next day.

It was great to have Father home. He'd been home for Christmas 1917, and a couple of other times as well. At the High School, Peter had boasted that his father had never been wounded; but he quickly stopped. Other men had scars, mutilations and decorations for their sons to boast of. Or graves in France. Arnold Cushnahan's brother had lost a leg at Ypres; Angus Igoe's uncle had lost both at the Somme; Simon

Reddington's brother's best friend had been awarded the Military Cross; Samuel McMorrow's father the same – post-humously. They all had relations who had partaken in heroic actions, charged against the German guns with no mean thought of personal safety, but for God and Ulster's sake. For King and Country. And they could prove their boasts.

Peter's father had no medals. He'd been very lucky. His only injury had been a broken ankle, and he had suffered that in leaping into a trench after the Huns had discovered a listening post and raked it with machinegun-fire, one night when a cloud betrayed the moon. He joked about this odd injury: a 'Blighty', no less!

Well, he used to joke about it – once, when he'd been home on leave. Now, when he was home for good, Peter noticed that his father didn't joke. He didn't laugh. He was a silent man. During the long weekend that Peter was allowed off school, his father prowled about the house like an uneasy animal. He spent a lot of time in bed. He didn't go down to the mill except once when this could not be avoided, dealing through McBride, his foreman.

'Your father's ill, children. Be quiet, please.'

On Sunday, after church, Peter finally got a moment alone with him. 'What's the most heroic thing you ever did, Father?'

'What?' The man sounded startled.

'In the war. What's the most heroic thing you ever did?'

His father frowned. 'What's heroic?' He looked puzzled.

Peter smiled. 'Ah come on, Father. You know.'

Trevor Gibson didn't smile.

'Please, Father. Tell me.'

'I saw a man once risk his life to save his chum.' There was something in the tone, or perhaps in the long pause that had preceded the reply, or perhaps in the way his father glanced over his shoulder, that disquieted Peter. 'I saw that same man prodded to the line at bayonet point. Dragged. Screaming. Was he a hero or a coward?' Trevor Gibson was staring. It seemed as if he didn't recognise his son. 'I don't know. I don't know what you mean. I don't know what – certain words mean. Not any more.'

Peter was disappointed. But perhaps Father was just being modest. Yes, that must be it. Self-praise is no recommendation. He'd often said it.

Back at the High School, between classes and games, between games and prep, in the dorm after lights-out, all talk and whispers were of the war and the armistice, and what sort of terms to put before the Germans, and whether they'd hang the Kaiser. Several younger masters, whom Peter had never known, returned to the school. Services were held in chapel for those who failed to do so. There were two new boys in Upper Sixth, who had fought in the trenches though they were only a few years older than Peter. They kept to themselves, or spoke to the masters man to man. The headmaster and the other, older teachers fêted their colleagues and the two youths, who all seemed embarrassed by the attention.

But the books in the library supplied details of all the heroism that the modest ex-soldiers left out of their sketchy accounts, on the rare times they could be inveigled to speak of the war. Peter borrowed *Private Pete* and read with fascination and disgust of the Germans' ravishment and mutilation of a young Belgian girl, of their crucifying a Canadian sergeant with bayonets. They were animals, plain and simple. Worse than animals.

Home for Easter, Peter spoke to his father about the book. He mentioned the Belgian girl and her missing arm, and hinted that he knew what else the Huns had done to her. His father's eyes flitted from place to place. He said nothing.

'But the most dreadful thing, Father, was a poor Canadian sergeant that they crucified with bayonets.'

His father snapped. 'That never happened!'

Peter was amazed at the denial – and its heat. 'Oh but it did, Father. I read it in the book.'

'It never happened. If you were to believe all you hear, son, you'd eat all you see.' Trevor Gibson paused, then added, 'And by Christ we swallowed plenty of the bastards' lies.'

Peter was shocked by such a dreadful oath. 'I'm afraid you're mistaken, Father,' he said stiffly. 'That certainly did happen. Private Pete actually knew the man they did it to. A friend of his has pictures.' He became magnanimous. 'Of course, you wouldn't have heard about it. It was in the Canadian sector.'

But Trevor Gibson had heard about it.

'It was in the Canadian sector. And it was in the American sector. And it was in the French sector. And it was in the Gurkha sector, and the New Zealand sector, and the Meerut sector, and every other bloody sector. And it was a sergeant, and a private, and a lieutenant, and a captain. But I've yet to hear the name of the man who was crucified with German bayonets. Throw that book away, son. You'll never read the truth in books.' He was red in the face and shouting, but now he lowered his voice. 'There were worse things done than that.' He lowered his voice even further, so that Peter could hardly hear. 'And we were just as bad ourselves.'

'Oh come on! What do you mean?' Peter raised his own voice – for just a moment. 'Pardon me, Father,' he went on respectfully, 'but I don't think that's a very patriotic thing to say.'

'Patriotism had nothing to do with it.' Trevor Gibson was staring at something; his voice was low and indistinct. 'Not at the finish. We all just did the best we could – to get through each day without being killed.' He looked at his son. 'You won't read that in books, but it's the truth.'

'Your father's ill, Peter,' his mother explained a short while later, when she found him moping in the foggy garden. 'You mustn't upset him.'

'I only spoke to him about the war. If it were me, I'd be proud to speak to my son about it.'

The woman sighed. 'Your father's ill.'

That night Peter discovered that this was a lie. He came down, late, to get a glass of milk. The house was silent, but as he approached the open door to the kitchen he heard a rhythmic creaking. By the faint light from the firebox of the range, he could see the housekeeper's armchair rocking.

'Nan?' he said softly.

There was no reply. Then he saw that Nelson, the retriever, had her head on the lap of the person in the rocking chair, and he heard a man's hoarse whisper. As his eyes adjusted, he saw his father's hand tugging one of the dog's ears between a finger and a thumb. He heard his father's voice.

'Oh why, Nellie, oh why.'

'Father?' Peter whispered.

Neither man nor dog gave any indication that they'd heard. The low whine of one seemed to be in answer to the other. Peter opened his mouth to speak again – more loudly; he left it open.

'As fine a morning as ever graced God's earth. Oh it was, Nellie, it was. How could God have sent such a day to follow?'

Nelson whined again, and looked mournfully up at the man, as though bewildered and bereaved as well.

A sick feeling crept over Peter as he watched the beings by the hearth. His open mouth was dry. There was something strange and terrifying, something fascinating, forbidding, about that rhythmic movement of his father's body in the chair – to and fro, to and fro; of his father's fingers along the dumb dog's ear – to and fro, to and fro.

'Why, Nellie, why?' Trevor Gibson's voice rose suddenly. The dog yelped and pulled its head away.

Then a bottle rolled across the tiles, making a hollow ringing noise. It stopped against the door, almost at Peter's feet. Peter was horrified. He knew what that bottle had contained. For now he could smell the disgusting reek of whiskey. His father was hunched up in the chair, crying. Like an old woman! Peter could hardly believe his senses. He crept away to bed and lay awake all night.

For the rest of the holiday, Peter avoided his father. It wasn't difficult. Trevor Gibson kept to his room, at best spent a few hours in his office. He spoke to McBride, but stayed away from the mill. Towards dusk he walked the land with one of the Purdeys in the crook of his arm. Once he brought home a hare, thin and stringy after the winter; but Nan hung and jugged it, and said her master was a mighty man. He didn't appear at the dining table. 'Your father isn't well, children.'

Back at school, the fearful thought took root in Peter's mind: his father was a coward. He'd blubbered like an old woman, that night in the kitchen. What shameful memory did that day, that God had sent, hold for his father? 'Why, Nellie, oh why?' Why *what*? Why had his courage failed to measure up? He'd actually compared himself to the Germans – 'We were just as bad ourselves' – and everyone knew that Germans were cowards. Private Pete had said that they were good fighters up to a point, but their cowardice was proved by their universal terror of cold steel. Why else would his father drink? Drinkers were cowards who couldn't face the challenge that God had placed before them in this world. That's what the Sunday-school teacher always said. They drank to forget their failure. What had his father done in France that he couldn't bear to remember? The answer was simple; there could be only one: he'd turned craven; funked it; shown the white feather. That was why he'd never been wounded. Or got a medal. He'd shirked his duty. His single injury had been sustained, by his own admission, when he'd been running away.

Home again for the summer holidays, Peter noticed the worry lines deepen in his mother's face, the small creases of contempt in McBride's whenever he came to the house to discuss business at the mill. There was an ugly sort of mood about the place, Peter overheard him say, and a fair few taking their flax to Treanor's to be scutched. Though sure what could you expect from papists, after that Sinn Féin business at the polls? But that was only a disguise for his contempt. Peter wished he were older. He'd wipe the sneer off McBride's face! He'd teach him to despise his father! And then he'd sort his father out. Tell him he'd just have to pull himself together, and cut out the blasted whiskey!

There was no whiskey on the table next Boxing Day, when Uncle Bob and Aunt Henrietta, and Uncle Sammy and Aunt Rachel, all came for their post-Christmas dinner as usual. But there was a watery eye in Trevor Gibson's head, and a slurred tongue in his mouth, as he said grace. Peter was old enough to dine with the grown-ups now. He was mortified – and hugely angry. He prayed that his father wouldn't make a total fool of himself – make fools of them all.

For a long time there was little conversation beyond 'Pass the gravy, please' or 'Goodness, Hannah, what delicious stuffing.' Then Uncle Bob said, 'Well, I hope we'll all be here at the same time next year.'

There was silence. Peter noticed his mother's mouth purse.

Uncle Sammy said, 'Sure why won't we! We beat them before at the Boyne, and we'll beat them again at the Fane. Ach go on, Hannah. Sure the lad must know. Are they talking about it at the High School, Peter?'

Peter glanced at his father. His father said nothing.

'About what, Uncle Sammy?'

'About the Fenians trying to take over? The papists? An Irish Republic?'

'I think,' Peter's mother said, 'you men can talk about this later. Among yourselves.'

Aunt Rachel and Aunt Henrietta nodded primly.

Peter was putting on pounds and inches when the War of Independence broke out. He didn't speak to his father now. Sometimes he dreamed of him, crouched in a dugout, in the attitude of Bully Murphy in the comic cuts: his bottom stuck up, his head drawn down, his hands over his ears, and a handsome officer – with swagger stick raised – above him. Come on Gibson, you dashed coward! On your feet. Do your duty. Be a man! McBride complained to Peter now of the fall-off in business at the mill. Troth he knew what he'd do with them! Every damn dirty papist in the country!

They were sitting down to dinner one evening during half term, in the latter part of that year, 1921: Peter, his mother, his brother and sister. His father, as usual, was 'ill'.

'Peter, would you say grace, please?'

Peter was pleased to be asked, and proud to oblige. He opened his mouth – then stared. Nan, the housekeeper, was stepping in from the kitchen. There were two men with her. Strange men.

'If you please, mam,' Nan said in a sort of croak.

The annoyance that Peter felt at this interruption changed quickly to a knot of fear in his guts. One of the men spoke.

'Mrs Gibson? I represent the Irish Republican Army. We're here to commandeer weapons to be used in the struggle for independence. You will be issued with a proper receipt, and the weapons, or their value, will be refunded when the struggle's over. Where's your husband?'

'He's ill. In his room.'

The man turned and called out. Two other men came in from the kitchen. One held a shotgun, the other a revolver.

'Go with this woman and get him,' the ringleader said to the man with the revolver. Nan, weeping, led the man away.

'Now, where are the guns?' the ringleader said.

'You'll have to ask my husband that.'

'I'm asking you, missus.' There was a sharp edge to the man's tongue. Peter plucked up all his courage.

'Don't you speak to her like that!' His voice sounded dreadfully high and squeaky. He felt himself blush. The ringleader ignored him, but the shotgunner turned to frown at him, and the twin muzzles of his weapon wavered in Peter's direction. Peter got a bad need to visit the lavatory.

'They're in the study,' his mother said. She led the way. There were the guns, in a glass-fronted cabinet.

'Where's the key?'

'My husband has that.'

They waited for a while. 'Sit down, missus,' the man said, civilly enough.

Mrs Gibson seated herself in her husband's armchair, with Edward on one arm and Victoria on the other. Both children were crying silently. Peter took a stand behind them. The ringleader leaned an elbow on the mantelpiece, and gawked around at the hunting trophies on the walls. He dug a clay pipe from a pocket and filled it. The shotgunner stood by the window, looking off down the avenue. The other man stared through the glass at the array of guns: the Ballard rifle Peter's grandfather had used to kill buffalo in Canada; the double Nitro Express his father had used to kill the tiger in India; the Vetterli that had come in on the *Clyde Valley*; the Lee Metford and the BSA; the Greener ten-gauge, the matched brace of

Purdeys, and the single-barrel twenty-gauge; the ancient matchlock musket that had helped win the Battle of the Boyne; the Luger pistol that some fleeing German must have dropped at Passchendaele.

The ringleader struck a match. A voice spoke from the doorway.

'Put down that gun.'

Everyone stared. Trevor Gibson had the fourth rebel in a necklock. He was holding the rebel's revolver in his hand. He was pointing it at the shotgunner. The shotgunner balked. He looked to the ringleader. The ringleader winced and dropped the burnt-out match.

'I used to be pretty good with one of these,' Peter's father said. The shotgunner put down his gun.

'Hannah, would you take the children out of here, please?'

Peter was bursting with pride, ashamed of the thoughts he'd entertained about his father. The four rebels were lined up before the mantelpiece, facing the wall, their hands clasped on their heads.

'You too, Peter.'

'What are you going to do with them, Father?'

'Go on, son.'

They went back to the dining room, though they couldn't think of eating. Mrs Gibson set the distraught Nan in a chair.

'We know it wasn't your fault, Nan. We know you had nothing to do with it.'

But Nan was a papist, Peter knew. Perhaps she had been in on it. It would be just like a papist! As McBride always said.

'What's Father going to do?' Victoria whispered.

'He's going to shoot them, stupid!' Edward said.

'Quiet, children.'

'Isn't he, Peter?' Peter made no reply. What *was* his father going to do? Deliver them up to the authorities, of course.

There was sure to be a reward. He was sure to have his name and his picture in the papers. 'Local war hero single-handedly captures rebel gang.' Wouldn't that be something to show the boys at school!

'Do settle yourself, Nan,' Mrs Gibson said. 'Have some tea. It will steady your nerves. No, no, I'll make it.'

'It's okay,' Peter said. 'I will.'

'Good boy.' His mother smiled at him, and turned back to Nan.

Peter went through the kitchen to the hall. The study door was open. He crept close. Three of the rebels were still at the fireplace, their hands still clasped on their heads. The ringleader was sitting sideways on one end of the desk, Trevor Gibson on the other. Their legs were crossed. The ringleader was talking.

'We're both soldiers. The position's very simple.'

Trevor Gibson was silent. He held the revolver loosely in one hand, its barrel resting on his thigh. The shotgun was where it had been dropped – dangerously close, in Peter's view, to the other three rebels.

'I was at Gallipoli.' The leader put a match to his pipe and puffed. He and Trevor Gibson looked at each other. 'It's nothing personal – just war.' The rebel paused. 'We're not on the same side now.'

Trevor Gibson was silent. Peter could hear his own heart beating.

'There's no shame in surrender,' the rebel said, 'when it makes no sense to fight on. You must know that.'

'You forget: I'm the man holding the gun.'

Good man, Father. You tell him!

'I'm not forgetting it.' The rebel struck another match and raised it to his pipe. He kept his eyes on the other man's face. 'What good is it to you?'

Peter saw his father flush. The rebel seemed at ease. A cloud of blue smoke rose from his pipe bowl.

'Look: you've lost this one. Face facts. You might get the six – for a while – but County Monaghan's ours.'

'Well by God it's not yours yet!'

'Maybe not.' The rebel drew on his pipe again. 'Maybe not in law. But – where's *your* law?'

Peter saw his father slump. His mouth felt dry.

'Let's talk terms,' the rebel said. 'Honourable terms.'

Peter's father sighed. Peter was feeling dizzy.

'Give us what we came for,' the rebel said, 'and you'll be left alone. You have my word.'

'What's that worth?' Trevor Gibson sneered. The rebel said nothing. He puffed on his pipe again. Trevor Gibson lit a cigarette. His hands, Peter saw, were shaking.

'Leave me the Purdeys. They were a present from my father.'

The rebel considered. Peter was feeling sick now; sick to helplessness.

'All right.'

'And your word, as a soldier, that not one finger will be raised against this house or anyone in it? Ever.'

Peter recovered. He rushed into the room. 'No, Father. You mustn't do this.'

All eyes turned on him. One of the rebels by the fireplace made a move, but the ringleader jerked a hand.

'I told you to stay out of here,' Trevor Gibson said.

'You mustn't do this!' Peter screamed.

'I'll do what I bloody well like! It's my house. Now sit down. Sit down, I said!'

Peter was furious. But he obeyed, overwhelmed by the anger in his father's voice, and by the presence of so many hostile men.

Trevor Gibson turned back to the rebel leader. 'Your word of honour as a soldier?'

'My hand and word to God.'

Peter's father placed the revolver on the desk. Peter spat at his feet. The rebels by the fireplace lowered their hands. The leader rose and stretched out his.

'Your word's enough,' Trevor Gibson said stiffly, his own hand by his side. He went to the gun cabinet and opened it, then stood aside. The rebels reached in. 'Leave those,' he said curtly. 'The two twelve-bores.'

'Leave them,' the ringleader said.

One of the rebels laughed. 'We may leave this too,' he said, hefting the matchlock.

The leader chuckled. 'You may. We're not that hard up. Have you a piece of paper?'

'What?'

'A receipt. The weapons, or their value, will be ...'

'Forget it.'

'What?'

'Just – just get out of here. Come on. Get out. You've got what you came for. Now leave my house, and don't come back.'

The rebels piled out, two long guns to a man, the leader stuffing the Luger into the waistband of his trousers.

Trevor Gibson turned to his son. 'I wish you'd done as I asked.' Peter just stared, his eyes filled with scorn. 'I know what you're thinking, son. I know you think I should have done – something else. But it's a fool who'll lose a war to win a battle.'

Peter couldn't speak. Off down the avenue, a motor car's engine started, then drew away.

'They're gone now. That's the important thing. We're safe.'

Peter found his voice. 'That? *That's* the important thing?'

'Of course. We're safe now.'

'For how long?'

'That man gave me his word.'

Peter laughed bitterly. But he could feel tears in his eyes. 'His word? A Fenian? A papist? And you believed him?'

'I took a soldier's word –' Trevor Gibson checked himself. 'Look son . . .'

'Don't talk to me!' Peter's eyes were streaming. 'Don't try to fool me that it was the right thing you did. I know what you are: a coward!'

'Son . . .'

'Don't talk to me! Don't try to tell me lies.' Peter was sobbing now. 'All the other boys – they've got heroes. You – you had them at your mercy. You could have . . . Oh, you could have been a hero too.'

'Trevor?' Mrs Gibson's voice sounded from the hall.

'Just a moment.'

'Is Peter all right?'

'Yes.'

Trevor Gibson closed the door. 'I did it, son, because there are more important things than – heroes.'

'What? Cowards?'

Colour rose to Trevor Gibson's cheeks. 'I know you can't understand now, Peter. But try to remember, will you, when I tell you . . .'

'Don't *talk* to me!' Peter shouted. He wiped a cuff across his eyes and sniffed. He got to his feet. 'Don't make yourself worse by making up excuses.'

'Peter! Peter, son, just listen to me. Please.'

Peter crossed the room and jerked the door open. His mother was outside, her face pale.

'Peter?'

Peter stormed past to the front door.

'Trevor,' he heard her say, 'is everything – ? Are you all right, darling? Did they hurt you?'

The door crashed on his father's answer.

UNDERNEATH THE SKY

IT WAS ONE OF THOSE DAYS THAT comes sneaking into the forepart of the year and tries to make you believe that summer has come early, and to stay. A false, malicious day, my father might have muttered, with a farmer's nose to the north – a 'pet day'. But hell, my old man was full of shit back then. It had been a clichéd Irish winter, dreary and damp and cold as a witch's tit, but when I woke on that Saturday morning in Dublin twenty years ago, the day was bright and cheerful – bright as it was in the poster of the Arizona sunshine and the gleaming chrome. Up there on my wall, jaws set and eyes shaded, Hopper and Fonda stared off into, I used to think, forever. Now – ? Well, when's the last time you saw an *Easy Rider* poster?

But still – it felt good back then. Even now, the memory can still feel good. And I'm not even drunk yet. Yes sir, it felt good to be alive that day, long, long ago, when I was more innocent than anybody could have told me, and my biggest problem was the price of petrol – the October war was still a recent thing – or my fuzzy lip. The happiest day of my damn life. The first of it, that is. I had a pretty nice flat, and a bike in the yard behind that was the finest in the land – in my eyes, anyway. My only care was what to do with all that shining sun.

I reached beneath the bed for inspiration, and picked up the open bike magazine and spread it on my chest and started to gum three Rizla papers together. I smiled. I had Sheila too, of course, the most recent and the most amazing of the lot. I'd seen her around college through first year and lusted mightily after her. But I was not the only one, and she was so far beyond us all that I'd never allowed myself even to hope. Film star material. Legs as long as a summer day, and just as warm and inviting; grey eyes a man could get lost in for a lifetime. Saint Paul would have burned for her. She was a year ahead of me, doing Business Studies – and she was going out with a guy who played for the college first fifteen.

Before last Christmas, at a drunken end-of-term party, I found him slapping her around in the kitchen. He was a couple of inches taller than me, broader and much heavier, a typical rugby player, with a glossy black beard which I resented almost as much as I envied him his girlfriend. When he turned around and yelled at me to fuck off, his face as red as beefsteak, the veins on his neck like Wavin pipes, I felt my knees go weak. But I'd had a few to drink, so I took him on. I beat him.

When Hilary term opened in January, Sheila started going out with me. Turned out she'd had her eye on me too. Nicest words I ever heard she murmured in my ear on our first night together: 'I knew you'd be good.' Now I sometimes wonder if she meant it. If she even said it. I was still too young to be much good. On a first night anyway. We were both drunk at the time.

But on that pet-day morning, I was innocent and gullible, and never let down by my manhood. I was afloat on a cloud, smiling like a fool at Hopper and Fonda, up there on their Harley-Davidsons, and at the memory and the flattery. And at the reality, still amazed, as I rolled up the reefer and took a hit off it. The radio alarm clicked, and music played. Beside me Sheila stirred.

'Morning, sweetheart.' I kissed her. She drew away and gave me a drowsy answer. I offered her the joint.

'At this hour?' she groaned.

'Hey. Love me, love my dog, right?' That's the song the radio was playing. 'Anyway,' and I winked at Fonda, who'd said it first, 'gives you a whooole nooo way of looking at the day.'

She grunted something cynical and crawled across me. I ran my free hand across her buttocks, down her thighs, back up between them.

'Cut that out.'

The touch of her, on top of the ganja, got me going, and I watched her twitch her naked tail the whole way to the bathroom. I finished the spliff. Couldn't help priming myself. When she got back to the bed I was dizzy with lust. She was languid making love – as usual in the mornings.

Later I speared the ragged remains of some cooked ham from the fridge. 'Fancy a bit of a pig's arse, my sweet?'

'Really, Liam, must you be so crude?'

'But I thought you liked talking dirty?'

'There's a time and place for everything, dear,' she said, wryly. As I folded the slithery meat in a slice of bread, she gave a delicate shudder. 'Really, Liam. Animal flesh for breakfast. You'll have a coronary before you're forty.'

'Will you nurse me back to health? Will you still need me, will you still feed me, when I'm sixty-four?'

She smiled, wryly again. 'How your inner man sticks the pace you set I'll never know.'

'How my outer man sticks the pace *you* set occasionally puzzles me. You just concentrate on him, honey, and don't worry about ma stomach. It can handle anything.'

She smiled again, more wryly than ever, at my imitation John Wayne accent. I think. Well, I used to think so. And maybe I was right. But I'm getting to that stage now where I can't be sure of anything.

She poured herself a bowl of muesli, and stirred thick yoghurt through it.

'So what do you want to do?' I said.

She shrugged. 'I'm easy.'

'Oh I know that. But what do you want to *do?* It's a cracker day. Be a shame to waste it.' I paused. 'How about that place you were telling me about in Wicklow? Your grandparents' place. You like to go there?'

She considered. 'Yes. Yes, that's a fine idea, Liam. You aren't just all brawn.'

I felt a wee, wee bit uneasy. I wasn't all that brawny. My beard was a disaster. I'd given up on it entirely. From time to time, I wondered about that rugby player. The few times I'd seen him this term I'd avoided him. Even when he'd been whispering to Sheila at the pavilion bar.

Not that I was afraid of him. I'd beaten him, hadn't I?

I thumbed my thin moustache. I had no need to worry. Sheila's smile was sincere. She was obviously interested.

'Yes, it would be nice to see the old place again. It's been – oh, must be ten years now. Haven't visited since Daddy died.'

I maintained a respectful few seconds of silence. 'Think you can find it?'

She frowned. 'I'd say so. It's just a few miles from Glendalough. We can enquire.'

I giggled; I was still light-headed from the smoke. The whole thing seemed a bit unreal: the day, the world, the girl, and even me. But that's what Mary-Jane can do for you – right? With booze you lose, with dope you hope, we used to say back then, when we were trying to cod ourselves that we were hippies. With women you never know.

We went down to the yard, togged out for the road. I'd spent a sobering amount of this term's grant on a leather jacket and a Ned Kelly helmet for Sheila. She'd protested. She'd been embarrassed and even annoyed.

'Look: if you're pillion on my bike, you're taking no chances. Right?'

Just the sight of that bike could cheer me up. A Moto Guzzi 850. Red as a gorgeous sunset. Low-slung and slab-sided. Powerful-looking in a past-it sort of way. Just two years old, it was outdated already, obsolete on the drawing board, its dynamo and drum brakes anachronisms, its vee-twin engine – a thirty-year-old design, lifted from an Italian army personnel carrier – sluggish and slow alongside any Japanese five-hundred. Even a good three-fifty. But man I tell you: I loved it. Damn near got a hard-on driving through the Dublin traffic, with that big thing between my legs and me between Sheila's and her tucked close behind me. The clatter of its pushrods, the whine from its timing chest, the greedy sucking through its tiny carbs as I accelerated to overtake, the twitter and snarl through its Gold Star pipes as I throttled back: music for the deaf. If they couldn't hear it they could feel it passing by.

Sheila and I slouched on the big mattress of a buddy seat, nonchalant and cocky behind our shades. Well, I was wearing shades. Small boys gawked at us from cars, flat-nosed, goggle-eyed and freaked out as they pressed against the glass. Their fathers, or their mothers, eyed us in their mirrors, wary, hostile. One woman rolled her window closed as I trickled past coming to a red light. A man hardly into his thirties – but that seemed ancient to me then – smiled in admiration.

'That's a beautiful machine.'

'Thanks,' I grunted, eyes ahead.

'What'll she do, mister?' a child called from the back seat.

His father laughed.

'What *will* it do?' he said.

I shrugged, fittingly blasé. 'Ton twenty. Ton twenty-five.' On a good day the Guzzi'd crack the ton. I'd been a little disappointed about that, but had forgiven her.

At my elbow, the man whistled. 'Lot faster than my old bus.'

I nodded and grinned at the distance. The light changed and I let her rip. Okay, so in a world full of Japanese fours the old girl was outgunned and outnumbered; sometimes she was outmanoeuvred; but she was never outclassed. Not then, not ever – Christ, I wish I had her now.

Sheila was laughing. 'You're loving this, aren't you?'

'Yeah,' I growled, John Wayne. Another light changed, and I gunned the engine and popped the clutch. The drive shaft tried to climb up the back wheel; the whole plot skipped to the side. The tyre squawked. Behind me a horn blared. I wagged a finger. I felt Sheila's tiny fists against my back. Over the snarl of the Goldie pipes, I heard her delighted laugh. I whooped with joy.

We spent quite a while looking for the old house. 'Farquharson? No one of that name hereabouts.'

'They moved to Dublin about thirty years ago,' Sheila explained.

Eventually we found it, up a wretched laneway, behind a locked gate. There were a few hairy bullocks moping in the muddy yard, splotchy with ringworm, hump-backed with hoose coughs; a few hay bales stacked inside the ruined house, more burst and scattered. Rats' droppings and fallen plaster. I liked the place. So eerie – the plaster crunching between my jackboots and the wooden floors. So isolated – a lovely melancholy blackness to the stand of pines on the slope beyond the ragged-slated roof. A primeval smell of damp earth and animals.

'It's not how I remember it at all,' Sheila murmured.

I kissed her. She shivered her head away and twitched her mouth. 'Why don't you shave it off? I liked you better without it.'

I'd been trying to grow the damn moustache for weeks. A few days ago, I'd met my previous girlfriend in the buttery and she'd said it looked great. 'Makes you look like Omar Sharif.'

'Let's give it another while,' I said to Sheila.

I led her round the back into the stand of pines. I laid our leather jackets on the ground. I opened her belt – she let me. I knelt down, eased her jeans over her hips, slipped her pants off, and kissed her there. She shivered again. I lay on the spongy pine needles and drew her down on top of me and we made love in silence. Hardly a moan. But I remember it was very beautiful.

It did feel sort of sacred out there underneath the sky. I've had a few to drink now, but it isn't my imagination.

I remember feeling cold when it was over. Above, beyond the dark loom of the pines, the clouds were as grey as Sheila's impossible eyes. She stood up off me and pulled her jeans on. I dressed myself. We didn't speak a word, I do believe, until we got to Glendalough, and we didn't go up to the lakes.

'Fancy a drink?' I pulled the Guzzi up before the Laragh Inn. I got a pint of Guinness and a Pernod and white for Sheila. We sat at a table and sipped. There was a fair crowd in the bar, excited, cheering, groaning; a rugby match on television. Ireland was playing Scotland. Sheila was interested. Her great-grandfather had been Scottish, she explained. She'd told me before.

'It was a good day, wasn't it?' I said – then flinched. She'd screamed right in my ear. Men were on their feet, roaring with delight. Ireland had just scored a try. 'Good stuff.' I grinned. Sheila was more excited than I'd seen her all day. Ireland won. She was delighted.

We had more to drink. It was gloomy when we left. It was cold. There was bad weather moving in. Well, it had been a powerful day.

I took the mountain road towards the Sally Gap, racing against the forecast, though I knew the view was gone. I got lucky. A few spits of rain, that's all. I was going handy. I'd had four pints of stout and was very conscious of my passenger. Of my responsibility. I was so determined to be worthy of her. I loved her so much. There was so much to live for – together.

A few miles from the gap, I got a glimpse of a headlight in my mirror. It was almost dark now. I shifted down as the light grew larger in my vision. The bike shot past. A Z1. Kawasaki 900. Top of the horsepower tree back then, in the mid-seventies. I wound the Guzzi's throttle wide.

We crossed the Sally Gap and hurtled down the mountains towards the bright lights of the city far away, together, sometimes a hundred yards and more between the bikes, sometimes a few lengths. I lost to the riceburner's awesome power and acceleration on the straights, gained a bit on corners, the Guzzi scraping steel and trailing sparks from the low-slung chassis, the 'curly' touring frame flexing like an overripe banana, the much-touted four-shoe brake not worth a toss after the first few hard applications. On balls and irreverent prayer. Coming into Tallaght – still a village then – I throttled back and flashed the headlamp a few times. The other man responded with a thumb-twiddle of his indicator switch, and a gloved hand raised in farewell. I chuckled. It had been as good an end to a sort of perfect day as I could have wished for. Realistically, given what I had, I couldn't have beaten the guy; but I'd worried him. Yeah, no one comes the dog with a man like me. Even if I'm outgunned and out-numbered – outmanoeuvred now and all – I can still outclass any son of a bitch. Any time.

That's the way I felt then. That's the way I still can feel. Looking back. In my cups. Now.

Then I felt Sheila shuddering behind me.

'Hey! Relax, woman. We're alive.'

We rumbled through the city.

'You want a drink?' I locked the Guzzi up in Trinity's bike park, and headed for the buttery.

As we were walking past the pavilion, Sheila said, 'Let's go in here.'

I hesitated. But what did I have to be afraid of?

There was a big crowd in the bar. The whole city was hop-ping after the rugby match. After a long wait, I got two drinks and came back with them to the table where I'd sat her down. Her ex-boyfriend was bent over her. She was saying some-thing, her eyes raised, her mouth slightly ajar, her throat taut as she leaned back to look up at him. The rugby player turned as I approached. First with his head, then with his feet. Then he walked to where a few of his mates were leaning against the bar. All big men like himself. All rugby players. All bigger than me.

I placed the Guinness and the Pernod on the table and sat down. 'What did he want?'

'Nothing. He was just apologising.'

I lowered about half the stout before I set the glass down. 'Is that right?'

'Yes.'

I looked over at the big guys. He – Sheila's ex – and one other man were looking back at me. I stared at them for a while, then at Sheila. 'He's getting a bit too fond of apologis-ing lately for my liking.'

'Liam.' I felt her hand upon my arm. 'Liam, please don't make trouble.'

We quarrelled. Back at the bike, she begged me to leave it. I refused.

'Well, I'm taking a taxi.'

'Suit yourself.'

'You're not fit to drive.' She took my arm. 'Please, Liam. Take a taxi.'

I pushed her off, then grabbed her back. Almost dropped the bike. 'Climb on. I'm not drunk.'

'No,' she said. 'I'm taking a taxi.'

'Oh aye? Who with?' She turned and walked away from me. 'Bitch!' I yelled after her.

I was lying on the ground, conscious of a certain feeling that was close enough to pain. There was something funny about my mouth. I thought it was she who'd hit me. Then I saw him there, up there, raindrops sparkling on his glossy beard, his big fists cocked. I put a hand to my lips, and tried to work my tongue. Then I tried to rise.

'You watch your mouth,' the rugby player said. I couldn't see where Sheila was. Again I tried to rise. The big guy put one foot on my chest. 'Stay down,' he said. 'I'm not drunk now.'

I knocked his foot away and clambered to my feet – he let me. I didn't land a decent punch on him. Two porters broke it up. I cursed them all; her as well. My tongue was working now, but bleeding. All my upper teeth were loose in front. A cold sleety rain was falling.

I think I called into the Yacht for more drink. I think I went looking for that big rugby player. I can't be sure. I can't remember getting home. It was my first blackout. When the radio alarm clicked next morning, some guy was saying Mass. I switched the damn thing off and hurled it across the room.

My hangover was brutal; my lips and tongue were swollen. And my right hand and knee were torn, and my hip hurt like hell.

I almost cried after I hobbled out to the yard. There was an inch of slushy snow on the Moto Guzzi's fuel tank and seat, but the dent on the tank was too deep to cover up. The mirror was smashed and flattened, the handlebars badly twisted. Thin veins of rust were already leaking through the chrome of one battered Gold Star silencer.

That day's like will never come again. I know that. I think I knew it even at the time.

The Guzzi's gone. Long gone. This drunk rode it right under a truck one night, way past the second axle, and didn't even have the decency to kill himself in the crash. I brought its remains home to the farm in a trailer, along with all my books, after I'd failed my exams. It lay in the corner of a shed for years, gathering dust each harvest time, crumbling into rust each winter. I swore, I swore, swaying on one foot in the middle of many a night, with calves bawling in fright at my drunken oaths and the beating of my crutch against the walls, I swore that some day I'd put that beautiful bike back on the road.

But of course I never did. That's obvious. You saw that coming – didn't you? Ten years ago, when I was really bad, I took a hundred quid for it, from this smiling, confident young guy with a gold filling. He wanted to plunder its timing gears for his new Mark III Le Mans. Guzzi started putting chains inside their timing chests when they dropped that old model of mine. They rattle now, like something from Japan, and eat themselves up from inside, because the tensioners don't work. They went to shit, like everything else, before the seventies were played out.

Sheila's gone as well. But of course you saw that coming

too. Long gone from me. A long long time ago. I could no more hold onto that woman than I could have beaten that Kawasaki over the Sally Gap. It should have been obvious, but I was young then and, as I say, no one could have told me how much I didn't know. Oh, we met a few times after that best day of my life. But that was all. The last time we made love is still that time behind that ruined house in County Wicklow, underneath the sky. She married that damn rugby player. I remember getting drunk when I heard. Didn't sober up for days. I remember cursing her. I remember that I didn't give a fuck about her.

That's not the way I feel just now. But hell, I'm drunk just now. And I've got to get to bed. Work in the morning. Can't afford to lose this lousy job. If you're forty and fading – and not even fast; and no such luck as a coronary, as Sheila predicted – jobs are hard to come by. Especially if you're a cripple. Sheila's in the past. Like that old Moto Guzzi. I know that. Truly I do. I never can get drunk enough to forget.

And I'm still swinging in here, man, like the ponytail that dangles down my back. Greyer and thinner every year. Like the balls on an old bull. Between a pair of crutches. Still swinging. But still fighting too. I'll be sober in the morning. I'll be in time to punch that card. Just you wait and see.

Women and men

Two days had passed now, warm, late-summer days, and no one could pretend for any longer that there wasn't something very seriously wrong. From where the two women stood, where a lane joined the road, the clamour from across the valley was loud.

'A mortal sin, that's what it is,' the older of the women spoke, 'to leave dumb animals like that.' Cows were bawling, pigs were squealing, a continuous, nerve-fretting noise.

'Do you think, maybe, she could have gone off again, and he after her?' The other woman was still young, in her twenties maybe, but it would have taken a second or a third glance to realise this. Her face was strained and haggard, her hair thin, unkempt, and streaked with grey. A wedding ring was her sole adornment. She was heavily pregnant. Four children played in the dust of the roadway, the youngest not a year old. Another child, a boy of maybe nine, was standing between the women, beside the field gate, looking off across the valley.

'If the fellow had any sense,' the older woman retorted, 'he'd let her go. Far better off without her.' This woman wore no ring. 'No, it's not that, Bridie. He would have come over to get our Jemmy to look after the stock for him, same as before. No.' Her tone was grim. 'They're there. The pair of them.'

'Do you think so, Maura?'

Maura didn't answer.

'I heard her say,' Bridie said, 'that as long as the Sacred Heart lamp was burning, she felt safe from him.'

'Ach. If she'd spent more time on her feet about the place than she did on her knees, she'd have been safe enough without a lamp.' Maura chuckled. 'Or more time on the broad of her back, maybe.'

'Wheesht. The child.'

The boy glanced up with only mild curiosity. He looked too wise for a child. The squealing of pigs reached a sudden, frantic pitch. The child turned his gaze back across the valley.

'They're eating each other,' he murmured.

There was a lengthy silence.

'What – what do you think, Maura?'

'I think, maybe the Sacred Heart lamp went out.'

'God forbid!'

'Troth, he was a quiet man, poor Dan Peadar. Too quiet for his own good – and for hers too, in song.'

'She was a good religious woman,' Bridie said. 'At confession every week, and at the rails every Sunday. Never missed a First Friday.'

'Aw a real Holy Joe!' Maura sneered. 'But what sort of woman would say what she said at Mona Myers' wedding? And what sort of a man would take it, only poor Dan Peadar? A soft man, in song.'

'She had a wee bit too much sherry, that's all. On the day that was in it.'

'And if you had too much sherry, would you say it? And if you did say it, sherry or no sherry, in front of our Jemmy, do you think he wouldn't break your jaw? And do you think he wouldn't be right? Troth, if it was any other man whose wife had said it, it's a funeral the priest would have had on his hands.'

'Wheesht!' the boy said suddenly.

The two women listened. The noise from across the valley had abated for a moment.

'What is it, Tom?'

'I hear my father coming.'

'God bless your hearing, *a mhic*,' Maura said.

Then, as the noise of the animals abated momentarily again, the women heard it too: the sound of iron-shod wheels and hooves. The boy ran off. The other children ceased their games, and clustered around the women. The frantic din grew loud again.

'What'll we do, Maura?'

'Somebody'll have to go over. It's long after time.'

They exchanged a look, Maura's solemn, Bridie's full of fear.

'Is Dan Peadar after murdering the Nun?' the biggest of the little girls asked shrilly.

'Shut up, you little trollop!' her mother snapped, and raised a hand. The child ran a few yards off up the laneway, giggling, fingering a snotty nose. 'God forbid,' the woman murmured.

The rumble of the laden cart was getting louder. Across the brow of the hill, the points of a pair of hames came into view; then the horse, head down, straining; and finally the cart. A man was sitting sidesaddle on one shaft, the boy congruently on the other, an old man's face on him.

The man reined in the horse beside the gate and stepped onto the road. He approached the two women leisurely, pulling a pipe and a plug of tobacco from the bib pocket of his dungarees. The women waited for him.

'No stir.' It was not a question. The noise from across the valley drowned out the snuffling complaint of pigs from the cart, over the splayboards of which a canvas winnowing sheet, weathered grey, was tied.

'No stir, Jemmy,' Maura said.

The man set the empty pipe between his teeth and blew through it a few times. He put his hand inside one bulging jacket pocket, and worked out a blood-stained corded package wrapped in butcher paper. He handed it to the younger woman. The woman took the meat without a word. He brought another package from the other pocket.

'Sausages. For the childer.' He handed that over too. 'You might set the pan a-squealing, woman. I had a long day of it on the fairgreen.'

Bridie took a step towards the laneway, but went no farther. Like the others, in her mind she was across the valley.

The man began to whittle at his plug. He was a big man, up on six foot, stout and heavy, with shoulders as square as a door. He might be forty-five, he might be more, though not a grey rib showed in the hair beneath his grubby cap. His black moustache was thick and bristling, and covered his upper lip completely. Stubble several days old grew on his cheeks and throat, so densely that the porter stains down the seams that framed his chin could hardly be seen against it.

His sister glanced at him, but didn't speak, and again they stared across the valley, towards the stand of ash and sycamore, impenetrably green, that hid the desperate homestead. The wife was behind them, silent.

The man shredded the tobacco between his palms, blew through his pipe once more, and took it from his mouth.

'Da?'

'Aye, Tom?'

'Do you want me to take the mare up?'

'Do that, son. Heel the cart up fornenst the stable door, and put them in there for the time being. Go handy, now. Don't hurt them pigs. Throw a bucket of water into the cart and brush it out. Leave the mare stand for a while before you let her near the trough. Take Packie there to give you a hand.'

The boy took the reins. The mare raised her head from the grass verge and threw the collar back with a thud and a rattle of draught chains. The two children led her off.

'Oh son?'

'Aye, Da?'

The man turned to his wife. 'Soak some bran in boiling water. Then throw half a can of oats intil it. I'll feed the mare later,' he added, to his son. Then he filled his pipe, lit it, and smoked for the best part of a minute.

'So – no stir?' he said to his sister.

'You've ears on you, haven't you?'

'I suppose I'd better take a look.'

His tone betrayed reluctance. When he set his foot upon a rail, his wife said anxiously, 'Watch yourself, Jemmy.'

The man made no response until he was standing in the field. Then he turned and threw his chest out.

'Watch myself, is it? On the likes of Dan Peadar? A kabogue of a man that would be bullyragged and bullied by a woman?'

'Well – you never know. He might be lying in wait. With a knife, maybe.'

The man turned his head and set his face across the valley.

'Take a stick itself, Jemmy.'

'Have you nothing to be at, woman? I spent a long day on the fairgreen. Get up there and set that pan a-squealing, like I told you.'

Bridie set off up the lane, at a rapid waddle, carrying the baby. Maura rested her forearms on the gate and followed her brother's progress down the brae, across the wooden plank that spanned the stream, and up the other side of the valley, until he was lost to view among the trees. The noise of the animals hit a fresh pitch of frenzy.

'Is my da going to get killed?' the little girl asked in her shrill voice.

'Wheesht, child!' The woman crossed herself and muttered something.

The sun sank lower in the sky. The children left their games and went home. The pigs stopped squealing; then the bawling of the cattle began to abate. Bridie returned to the vigil site. Neither woman spoke. The sun was poised above the horizon, the valley silent now but for the sound of children's laughter and, overhead, the cawing of a cloud of rooks bound for the grove below the mountain. Suspended in the air were the smells of a late-summer evening: warm dung and dust, saved hay and, from somewhere downstream, the stench of rotting flax.

'Well, his dinner's on the hob, and if it's cold by the time he gets back, I don't know what I'm going to do.'

Maura made no answer. The two women peered across the valley.

A man stepped out from between the trees and began to make his way downhill. When they could distinguish his gait, the women said in chorus, 'Thank God!' They said no more until Big Jemmy came up to them.

'Well?' Maura asked.

Big Jemmy turned his back on the women to rest his elbows on the top rail of the gate, and looked back the way he'd come. He took his pipe out, blew through it, and filled it carefully. He shook his head.

'Well?'

'Never seen the like of it in all my days. Not since God put the breath of life in me.' He lit the pipe and puffed on it. He shook his head again.

'Are they – there?' Bridie asked.

'Not since God put the breath of life in me. The pigs were

eating each other. There's two of them dead, and another that isn't going to do. Milk running out of the cows' tits onto the ground. The suck-calf's dead in the shed. Never seen the like of it in all my days.' He shook his head again. 'I should have gone over last night. Or first thing this morning, before I set off to the fair.'

'Now Jemmy, there's no one wants to come between a man and his wife without good cause,' Maura said. 'It's not your fault.'

'Did – did you see any sign of them?' Bridie asked.

Big Jemmy shook his head. 'No sign. The door was locked, and the curtains pulled. But there was a bad class of a smell. And I could hear rats squealing in the kitchen. And there was blood on the doorstep, and a lot of it over by the washtub.'

Bridie began to whimper. Maura crossed herself and moved her lips.

'I shouted,' Big Jemmy said, 'but there was no answer.'

'Himself too, then, Jemmy?' Maura said quietly.

The man struck a match and held it to his pipe. He puffed until the tobacco lit. He fumbled in his pocket.

'I found these in the washtub.'

He turned to face them and reached his hand through the gate. The sun had set now, but in the gloaming the women could see a set of false teeth on the outstretched palm, with brownish smears dried on them. The blood might have been from the butcher meat, but the palate plate was broken in two.

'Oh, he killed her, the villain!' Bridie wailed. 'He must have killed her. God have mercy on her.'

Big Jemmy took the pipe from his teeth. He looked across the gate, past the women, up the laneway, towards the sound of happy laughter.

'He must have,' he said. 'He must have. God forgive her.'

HORNS OF A WHIMSICAL EDEN

DAMN THE BITCH! He could live without her!

Ralph McAuley threw his bulk into the Volvo and slammed the heavy door. He turned the key and floored the pedal. The engine roared. He clutched and rammed in first gear as though mashing Bridget's head against the dashboard, imagined the feel of fragile face bones breaking. The clutch bit and gravel spurted from the tyres. The back end of the big 244 fishtailed ponderously – as elegant as a performing hippopotamus, she had always described his car. Bloody bitch! At least it was a proper car. Ralph blasted the horn, and drove through the gate and onto the road without pausing.

After a few miles he cooled a little. The redness that tinged the hedgerows and road verges faded from his vision. He slowed to a pace to suit the worn surface of the road. Another mile or so and that pace was almost leisurely. A short while later he felt like chuckling – but could not quite manage that.

Though it was funny, he knew. It was downright funny the game they played, as though they hadn't a titter o' wit between them – as though they were children. There was no big deal. 'My girlfriend and I have been needing a break from each other for a while,' Ralph spoke aloud, as though addressing a child. 'We do so regularly. Why the big fuss? Why the stupid game?'

That's what it was, of course: a game – for both of them. Almost a ritual. It was simple when he articulated it aloud. He knew this. Always he knew it after the big flare-up had fizzled out like a damp squib. Yet he could never see it building up to ignition. It was as though – as though it was a game that he as well as she *wanted* to play. And like every game it had its rules.

Possibly the first rule in their game of living together was that conflict must always lurk like a mischievous playmate somewhere in the background. It might be true that opposites attract, but in their case they were both so competitive and ambitious – and so disparate – that rivalry was like the ghost at the feast; even though they rather despised each other's respective fields of scholarship. Between rivalry and contempt, it was remarkable that an art historian and a mathematician should find enough solid ground on which to build a home.

But they'd grown a lot through the games they played – he certainly had. The rows were far less frequent nowadays. The last big one had occurred just before they'd moved to the countryside, and that had been at the start of term last year. That had been a bad fight – the worst of all, Ralph remembered, a little ashamed still. He'd hit her that time. They'd both been certain it was over. He had moved out into Peter's flat, but so final had it seemed, so devoid of even basic respect had they apparently become, that he had paid the deposit on another flat and lived in it for a week. They'd met each other many times on campus, and exchanged a couple of frigid glances when it would have been fatuous to look the other way; later hardly less frigid nods, until after a few of these they'd been unable to keep their faces straight and suddenly laughed at the absurdity – and from love, of course – and rushed into each other's arms, in full view of other staff and students. He'd actually dropped his briefcase!

Yes, he loved her. Ralph felt a thrill that both warmed and

irritated him. But he needed to get away from her intense fussy nearness every so often. Needed to get drunk with the boys, screw around a little in Salthill, or in his old haunts in Dublin or back home in Belfast. She needed the break too, from his bouts of withdrawn moodiness or cerebral preoccupation, his cold sarcasm which could infuriate her as much as his usual jocular optimism. She needed to get back with her old AC-DC friends and bitch about men, and bemoan not having taken their advice and stayed far away from that male chauvinist bastard Ralph McAuley.

Somehow it always seemed to be she who came off second best after they'd made up. It was indeed, Ralph thought not ruefully, a man's world. Somehow after they re-established themselves together, for all that they both made concessions, and for all that he genuinely didn't do it maliciously, he seemed to be better off every time. It was never obvious immediately, and it wasn't one-way – he did pay a price – but probably a lot of the trouble stemmed from her seeing, after time had given her perspective, how she'd been outflanked in the peacemaking.

It had been she who'd suggested the move to the country: the stress of the city was their problem, or a good part of it. He'd agreed eventually. Yet in the end she lost out there too. It was her wish to move back to Galway that had precipitated the arguments of the past week – or provided the excuses. He liked the country now, Ralph had claimed affably – which was true enough, but he would probably have been willing to accommodate her. The knowledge that he'd seen through her spurious justifications for not renewing the lease had fanned the heat of her pre-menstrual temper, until today it had flared into sudden inferno over who should wash up after Sunday lunch.

Ralph swung the car onto a byroad. In real truth he did like

the countryside, and part of his reluctance to move back to the city stemmed from annoyance at himself for having seen so little of it in the year they'd lived here. It had been a busy time for both of them, of course, with the extra-mural courses she was taking, and the senior lectureship he was working towards. He was glad now to explore, and had a couple of hours to kill. He'd driven past the turning to the pier, but chances were this road would also take him onto the lake shore. He'd spend an hour or so down there, just walking and thinking and skimming stones. Later he'd hit the city and book Peter's couch for a few nights, and they'd go on the town if Peter hadn't too early a schedule tomorrow. Certainly they'd have a few pints in Naughten's or the Quays or Mick Taylor's, after the pubs opened at four.

Within a mile, verges began to intrude, and moss to grow between the tyres. Hedgerows closed above the car. Ralph throttled back, his eyes hunting for a farm gateway in which to turn. But the only houses were ruinous tumbles of ivied crumbling walls and tumbled thatch, entrances closed by stone walls or barbed wire. He drove until the surface all but gave out and the hedges were brushing the car, before resigning himself to a long ride in reverse to get out.

But he didn't mind. There was plenty of time, and here wasn't such a bad place to waste an hour. He stopped adjacent to a rusty gate and got out. It was a pleasant day: cold, but crisp and bracing after the stuffy heat of the car. He decided to leave the anorak – it was his good one. He was wearing an old tweed jacket and jeans and a pair of Doc Marten's, having spent the morning clearing the dead jungle of pea vines from the garden they'd begun with such enthusiasm last year. A brisk walk would dispel the chill and provide good exercise, and it wouldn't matter if he got dirty. He could change at Peter's place.

He grabbed the top bar of the gate and braced himself to vault across, but thought better of it. He wasn't such a young man any more, and the gate felt ready to fall. Lank yellow grass, killed by autumn frost, drooped across it, and the bottom bar, where it rested on the ground, like the hinge in the heelstone, was fretted with rust. He climbed cautiously across and set off uphill towards a rocky knoll covered by brush and scrubby trees.

The ground was moist, the grass drenched by the thaw of afternoon. The wood's dank smell was pleasant and evocative. Ralph recalled holidays on his grandfather's farm in Antrim: the bluebelled glens in spring, the rocky places that had been his hideouts in summer, icicles dripping on the eaves in winter. Really, the countryside was a grand place to live, and he wondered if he shouldn't go home and, sincerely this time, try to persuade Bridget to stay. Often he'd felt so refreshed on a Monday morning if they'd spent the weekend on the lake, or roaming the laneways, or even gardening.

She was so stubborn, though, that he had to go through with it. He had to play the game by its rules, if out of nothing but respect for both of them – indeed for the game itself. And he was looking forward to that brief taste of his bachelor days again. Midweek, however, he'd return; it would be short and sweet this time.

Perhaps he'd cut it really short this time. Have one or two drinks with Peter and come home tonight. Not so late that she'd have gone to bed, but about supper time. For all her justifying and all her sophistication, the real reason she wanted to go back to the city was because she was scared of the dark and the isolation. She was like a child in ways. She needed his protection. She needed a man, and it was the need for that need that might be what made him love her. She'd be missing him tonight, and it would be easy to make up, share

a bottle from their modest wine cellar and go to bed.

Why, he wondered, getting horny at the thought, was it always so much better after making up? Was that another reason why they fought?

The scrubby wood grew on a limestone crag, an ancient reef on which the teething seas had gnawed long before dinosaurs were born. Useless for farming, it had been left in a primeval state, covered by hazel, rowan and birch, colonising species that would have harried the heels of the ice sheets, caparisoned with threadbare patches of stunted blackthorn, the occasional hawthorn or larger tree growing where it could. It seemed not to have been touched by the hand, or even the foot, of man. But this, Ralph knew, was fanciful. Cattle roamed it, as their splashes of wet dung attested, and goats or perhaps deer had left pellet droppings along the paths and stripped the bark from many trees, activity that had resulted in small clearings here and there, with some skeletal limbs still standing. A few of these clearings were large enough to provide rough grazing. But there was no sign of active human interference. The only footprints in the mud were cloven-hoofed.

He was a little surprised. He would have imagined a place like this to be a lodestone for the yokel oafs who so ruined peaceful Sundays with the blasting of their guns. He kept an eye out now, but not one spent cartridge case did he spot. It seemed odd.

Then it struck him that this must be Carrigaphookha: the Rock of the Pookha, or devil. Ralph hadn't heard the legend behind the name but he could guess – there were hundreds of such legends all over rural Ireland. He smiled at the thought that in this day and age young men, who would no doubt feign cynicism and scorn for such matters, would none the less shun prime hunting grounds because of a suggestive name. Really the Irish were a gauche and superstitious race, even as

Europeans in 1995. Ralph regarded himself as an Ulsterman and British – and was quite proud of it, for all his broad-mindedness and appreciation of Irish music and culture; an Ulster Protestant behind his atheism. If he himself felt anything at being in so sinisterly named a place, it was a momentary and delicious thrill.

It was indeed a thrilling, eldritch place! It seemed primeval in a suggestive as well as literal sense. Rocks were everywhere: slippery polished outcrops underfoot; thickly mossed boulders piled on each other in sometimes fanciful shapes in the twig-filtered watery sunlight; treacherously flagged pavements, mossy or bare, split and tilted by tree roots. Some yellow leaves hung limply from the hazels and dropped to the ground as he brushed the branches; a few red berries that had escaped the birds and beasts dangled from rowans and hawthorns; here and there the brilliant russet of a crispy beech stood out. The dull brown of bark and withered bracken, spattered with dead briar leaves, bright as arterial blood, and the dark moss and purple blackthorns, formed a background. The effect, with the sun now sinking, was an odd, sombre cheerfulness. Its calm was in a way in keeping with its odd excitement. Once when he came to a small clearing Ralph harkened and from far away he could barely hear the sound of traffic on the road; a few yards back into the brush all was silent as – yes, the grave. He shivered with that delicious thrill.

Even the birds were silent, and he thought this rather odd until he realised that they were far outside their mating season, and that many would have migrated. It wasn't as though they'd all fled: once or twice a magpie or starling chattered narkily at his approach, or a pigeon noisily broke cover and flapped frantically away, causing his heart to thump. Ralph regretted not having discovered the place earlier. He could imagine how it would be to bring Bridget on a picnic here in summer. He felt his breathing change. It would be all but dark beneath the thick leaves then; cool, but warm enough to cast their fig leaves off in this small unclaimed Eden. And after a few glasses of good wine, wouldn't it be altogether too pagan and priapic to . . .

To hell with the pint in Naughten's! Ralph turned on his heel and set his face for home. There was a time for peacefulness and all that, but there was more to life than contemplation too. The pathways through the brush diverged, converged, entangled, and he was more engrossed with his destination than his journey, so that he had gone some little way before he realised that he was – not lost, but not quite certain where to turn.

He was not in the slightest worried – a little peeved at the delay. Briefly he thought of backtracking, but dismissed the notion, and went on.

A short while later he started looking for a clearing. From there he could gauge the sun's position and, by ear, the direction of the road, and move towards where the car would be.

Oddly though, he failed to find a clearing. So he decided simply to walk in a straight line – or as straight a line as the crooked pathways would permit. The wood was bigger than he would have thought, but it couldn't be all that big; a hundred or so acres in extent at most, he felt sure. In ten or fifteen minutes he was certain to come out of it, get his bearings, and circumvent it back to the car.

He looked at his watch. It was then that apprehension hit him. It was after four o'clock. Where had the time gone? He peered at the second hand, raising his wrist close to his eyes; the watch was fine. His apprehensiveness was heightened when he realised that in an hour or less it would be dark. But then, and in a way that whimsically disappointed him even as it relieved him, he saw a human footprint.

Relief was not even fully realised, for the footprint was his own.

The worry that punched him softly in the guts transmuted – logically – into impatience and mild self-directed anger. It was absurd that he should be lost in a little wood of a few acres, a man of his intelligence and worth. It wasn't as though he was in a wilderness. Of course he wasn't lost! He was less than twenty miles from Galway, a cosmopolitan city, one of the largest in the country, the fastest-growing in Europe. He was a rational man, a clever man. A measured genius in fact. It was a foregone conclusion that he'd be professor by thirty-five, arguably head of the department by forty. It was preposterous that he should be lost as a bumpkin on an outing to the town, in a civilised, thickly populated country.

He shivered. He was cold. Had been cold for some time, but hadn't liked to admit it. He berated himself for not having brought the anorak, then told himself to buck up. At the first chance he broke off at a tangent from the circular path he'd been beating.

From somewhere, far away or near at hand, just as his composure was returning, he heard a noise. It was the noise of a beast, one of the cattle of whose evidence he'd seen so much. But it was not a comforting sound. The low phlegmatic growl was that of a suspicious or angry bull.

For several seconds Ralph stood motionless. The noise seemed to come no closer, though it was difficult to judge its precise distance or direction. But his courage rallied. He was safe from such a threat as this anyway: bulls couldn't climb trees! He snickered at the mental image, then broke a stick off a hazel, his heart choking him at the loud snap and at the way in which the noise stopped the throaty rumble dead. But at once the low din commenced again.

The noise was ominous – diabolical was a word that elbowed

its way into his mind and refused to be dislodged. He made a decision on whence the noise was coming and went the other way – quickly. The route took him over one of the rough pavements, and several times he slipped on the slithery damp moss; but he hurried on.

It was more than gloomy now within the wood. Darkness was coagulating. It was impossible to deny fear by this time. When the face appeared he screamed.

He only got a glimpse of it, for he turned at once and fled. It had seemed to materialise in front of him; had he reached out he could have touched it. The only warning had been the pungent smell. Ralph ran, whimpering, back the way he'd come. As a logical man he knew that the bearded face with the huge horns sweeping up and back and sideways belonged to no more diabolical a being than a goat. But there had been something about the eyes, large and lustrous in the gloom, curious, intelligent and unafraid – malignant even – that musky stink, and the fact that the face had appeared so suddenly and at a level with his own; something that stripped raw an archaic nerve that stretched back far beyond the Reformation and the time of Christ to when his savage antecedents feared demons and pookhas and shivered about a fire and piled brush high to keep the darkness at a distance.

He was hardly assured by the tangibility of the apparition. He did not know how dangerous a large billy goat could be. He doubted that it could kill a man as a bull could, but he felt sure it could inflict significant injury. This was the rutting season and – he accounted for the level of the beast's head and its sudden appearance – the goat had reared up in aggression, perceiving the man as an intruder to be despatched. Terror drove the man, and drove out of his mind all thought of treacherous footing, all feeling of branches and thorns as they slashed at his face.

A flat rock tilted beneath him. His foot slid under the rock adjacent. His legs splayed. Pain tore at his groin, skewered him in the ankle. He sprawled on the mossy tumble. The pain contracted for an instant to a pinpoint of primal energy. A flashbulb burst behind his clenched eyelids. But above the rumble of the rocks Ralph had clearly heard a snap, and he knew that his leg was broken.

He could have been unconscious for no more than a few minutes, for it was still not fully dark when he came to. He was held fast, in the most excruciating pain he'd ever known. It made him gasp then scream and sob. His face and hands were lacerated. His temple had been split where he'd struck it in his fall, and blood was in his eyes. His left wrist was sprained and already swollen, the palm flayed. He'd torn a muscle in his groin or maybe even herniated. But worst of all was his right foot. It was clamped between the two rocks, caught in the jaws of an enormous natural trap. It was all but impossible to move, for the slightest attempt brought on such torment that nausea and unconsciousness threatened again.

He called for help – or began to. But even the small movement of filling his lungs and raising his head to shout caused the blackness to loom in threat. He reconsidered, fighting down his panic, urging himself to be calm: He'd be okay; it was just a goat. He shifted, gingerly, to a position that better accommodated his body among the stones, took deep, deliberate breaths, and examined himself.

The broken bone had bulged the flesh above his ankle, but had not split the skin. That was poor comfort. He felt baffled at the extent of his plight. It was such uncanny, malefic luck to have incurred such ruinous injuries. And it wasn't just his injuries: it was quite impossible to spring the trap. The rock slab was perhaps a quarter of a ton in weight, and completely immovable from where he lay. His efforts merely tore off

moss and quicked his fingernails. He cast about for something to use as a lever, but there was not even a rotten twig
within reach.

There was no good face to put on his position. He was isolated and helpless, up to a mile from any house, and possibly
more. No one knew where he was and it would be tomorrow
at the earliest before he was missed. The car might rust away
before anyone came on it by accident, and even after a search
was launched it could take days before it was discovered. But
of immediate import was the fact that he was helpless and
grievously incapacitated, with a cold winter night drawing
down. If he survived exposure there would be septicaemia
from the broken bone. And there were other dangers: if the
bull came on him, aroused by rut and the smell of blood ...
Or that – that goat-thing ...

He cried in pain and self-pity and frustrated anger. There
must be something he could do! He was a genius, it was impossible that he could not find a way out of this. He had so
much to do with his life; it was impossible that it could – oh
it couldn't end like this, so ludicrously pointless!

A fox would chew its leg off to escape such a trap. Ralph
laughed with weak hysteria, then broke off, screaming in
agony at the tiny involuntary movement he'd induced. He
used to make jokes about 'foxy women', women who'd
looked beautiful the night before, but who the morning after
would make a man chew off the arm about their necks rather
than risk waking them. He gave the idea serious consideration;
but he didn't have even a penknife.

He was desperately cold now and soaked from the damp
moss, so cold that the pain was becoming anaesthetised. He
had gained a more accommodating position and was able to
fill his lungs and shout.

'Help!' He paused, afraid, but there was no rattle of hard

hoofs on stones. He called again. 'Help! Help! Oh God help me, please!'

He could almost see the sound waves being absorbed by the dead leaves and moss as by a sponge. He wept and pleaded, 'Save me, someone! Bridget! Oh Bridget!'

As he was coming through the gate she was leaving by the door. She walked briskly past him, her gaze severe and businesslike ahead of her. He reached out as though through sun-warmed honey, but he couldn't touch her.

'Bridget!' His tongue was thick, and filled his mouth, got stuck between his teeth.

She didn't turn. She got into the car – his car, the Volvo – started it, and drove away.

He woke, sobbing. 'Oh you bitch! You Fenian bitch!'

It was dark as the inside of a deconsecrated church now, and the sky between the branches overhead was crammed with a legion of celestial eyes, glittering maliciously. Ralph no longer felt cold though he was shuddering like an epileptic. His pain was far away, his terror strangely dull. Sensation was slipping from him, but he knew that he had fouled himself.

He began to do something else now that he hadn't done since childhood.

He began to pray.

Unconsecrated ground

Ned Barrett called that morning when Paddy Joe Fahy was loaded up with seed. Wouldn't go into the house, though Maureen offered the sup of tea. Oh no, in too much of a hurry. Wouldn't say, though, where he was going or what his hurry was, and Paddy Joe wouldn't give him the satisfaction of asking outright. Not in so much of a hurry, either, that he didn't hang around till it got bright – giving a hand, by-the-way. Paddy Joe would have had the few wee jobs done quicker himself. Had to watch Ned like a hawk. Nosy wee know-all. But what could a man do? Neighbour from across the hill. Couldn't fall out over what Ned would be sure to report had been just a joke, and could Paddy Joe not have a bit of a laugh at himself?

'Aye, aye' – the snout stuck over another half door – 'not a bad litter. Eight. No? Ah well, if you want to call yon yoke a pig. I wouldn't. You'll do all right if she keeps eight. But tie knots on their tails, like a good man, or they'll get out through the cracks in the door.'

'Sow was off her grub,' Paddy Joe explained. 'She had eleven, but lost her milk. Had to get the vet. Didn't eat a bite for near a week.'

'And was she in the habit of eating, Paddy Joe?'

Cuttin' bastard. But we could all talk if we liked. Suit you better to keep your own side of the hedge trimmed. Think your own cattle weren't turning the stones looking for grass last March. Going round the fields on sticks, they were that weak with hunger. Think the country had a short memory? Paddy Joe didn't forget the brother Ned had buried on the wrong side of the graveyard wall, though he'd been no more than a *gasún* when the talk of the shame was going round. Course they put it out at the time that the fellow wasn't right. Astray in the head over something he'd seen in France. But Canon McCamley was a match for all the Barretts in the country. Wasn't the Great War over years ago, and hadn't we all our wee crosses to bear? Where would the world be if we all let life get us down, instead of down on our knees? Troth he wasn't the man to make little of decent Catholics who'd never doubted the mercy and goodness of God! He'd as soon bury a black pagan alongside them in the graveyard, as any man who'd hacked his throat open with a razor. Sooner, for it mightn't be the poor pagan's own fault he'd never get to heaven. So Michael Barrett lay in unconsecrated ground with other suicides and stillborn babies, and neither cross nor stone to say he'd ever lived and died.

And Paddy Joe Fahy knew all about it.

And if Barrett's brother didn't mind his manners, Paddy Joe would cast it up to him, neighbour or not.

'Ah dear oh!' Delighted now; sorry-for-your-troubles like. Ned had found the load of seed potatoes, the cart's shafts hung by the backband from a rafter. 'And Saint Patrick's Day come and gone' – shaking the wee ugly head. 'Sure any man hasn't his spuds planted now is late.' Maureen was passing on her way from the henhouse, so Paddy Joe held his tongue.

'Still,' Ned went on, 'better late than never. And going by the hill you managed to put on that woman of yours, you'll have plenty of help in a lock of years. I'll send one of mine over after school to give you a hand.' Another wee dry rub – *one* of them, like.

And off he took himself then, with plenty to report, and still without a word about where or what his own business might be.

But now it was mid-morning, and not even a rood of seed dropped, and still a long way from the scholars getting out of school. It was good times for Irish Free State farmers right enough. Every crumb of corn, the smallest spud that they could grow, the meanest beast that they could raise, would have a market. As far as Paddy Joe was concerned, Hitler could batter the shite out of Churchill and welcome – the longer the better. But the Emergency wouldn't last forever. And the money still had to be worked for.

He glanced over his shoulder. 'Get a move on, woman!' he muttered. Aloud he shouted, 'Hup!' The horse turned along the headland. Paddy Joe let go of the handles to rest. The plough fell onto its side, and dragged along.

Halfway up the field, his wife straightened from her stoop and flexed her back. In profile against the raw March sky, the jute-bag apron full of seed potatoes added to the swelling of her belly. She reminded him of the enormous cow he'd gone to marvel at one time, her calf-bed crammed with two bull calves and a heifer, all born healthy and sold for good money in due course. Remembering that he smiled into the slicing wind.

He hupp'd the horse again and carefully positioned the plough. He called 'Come up!' The horse strained against the collar, the sock slid into the ridge, and the twin mouldboards spread the soil over the drills on each side, covering the seed where it lay on ripe manure.

Close to the top headland he came abreast of the woman, a

half-dozen drills off, bent again to her task, reaching a split and budded potato from the coarse apron and placing it a forearm's length from the last. On the headland, she'd fill the apron from one of the bags Paddy Joe had placed there after Ned had left, and before he'd helped her gain a start on the plough. After he covered all the seed, he'd loose-out the horse for a couple of hours' rest and help Maureen.

Paddy Joe glanced at his woman and her belly as he passed her again on the way down. It ought to be a big strong child to go by the size of her. Please God it would be a boy.

As he looked, the woman straightened up, pressed one fist against a kidney, and arched her back. Ah dambut-skin, now! How many times was that? God knows, Paddy Joe was no slave driver. He made allowances – a man had to for these things. He knew better than to put one in shafts after getting her horsed, but a good mare would work in traces up to the hour she dropped the foal. Paddy Joe knew these things. He hadn't asked Maureen to load the dung or manhandle the heavy bags. But she was a while from her time yet, and well fit to drop seed. He was beginning to think that she was dragging too much out of a good thing.

'Are you all right?' he shouted. She nodded. 'Good, then get a move on!' he growled – but to himself. She was a good woman, who knew her place as well as he knew his, and the value of a ha'penny. But she was as slow as a funeral lately. He'd seeded three drills to every one of hers this morning.

He finished ploughing down again. Looking for her on the way back up, he didn't see her. He supposed she was refilling the apron from one of the bags across the crest of the hill. Turning the plough on the top headland, he glimpsed cloth fluttering in the wind. He found her on the ground, between two ridges. Her face was pale and sweaty. Paddy Joe was frightened – even more so than he was ashamed to be near her at this time: she was about to drop the child.

'Run!' she said between her teeth. And Paddy Joe ran. He ran to the headland, unhitched the traces, and tied the horse to a bush, at a safe distance from the nearest bag of seed – wouldn't do to have a valuable animal gorge and founder. He slipped the bit out of its mouth to let it graze. Then he ran to the house, and got on his bicycle.

When he got back, with Eiley Barrett on the crossbar, sniffing in his ear the whole way, his wife was crawling across the farmyard. From behind, Paddy Joe could see that her skirt was soaked with blood. Together he and Eiley carried her inside the house and to the bedroom. He waited in the kitchen. He knew that he should go back to the field, and was ashamed to be so close to a woman at her time, but he was too anxious and excited to leave.

He didn't hear a whimper till the child cried. Good woman; God bless you. He was desperate to be off then, before Eiley found him, but still anxious. Was it a boy, or was it a child?

It was a child, Eiley informed him – with a smirk, he didn't doubt. Very small, but healthy.

'Aw.' Paddy Joe heard the disappointment in his voice. He went on, defiantly, 'Well, she's welcome. She's welcome in this house – as welcome as the flowers of May, God bless her. Thank God.'

Then he noticed that Eiley was as jumpy as a hen on hot bricks. 'Is everything all right?' he asked.

Eiley coughed and sniffed. 'She wants you in there.'

Paddy Joe hesitated, feeling his face flush. 'Ach – she's all right.'

'She wants you,' Eiley muttered. 'Go on.'

Paddy Joe slunk towards the room door and went inside. He could imagine Eiley's gossip in the shop that evening to the women, and the men's necks craning in the bar behind.

'Close the door,' Maureen whispered. Paddy Joe hesitated. 'Close it!' she insisted. Paddy Joe did so, thinking of the juicy gyp they'd all knock out of this. 'Bejaysus could Fahy not wait till the woman got her breath back?' And the dirty guffaws.

Maureen signalled urgently; Paddy Joe came close. 'Take the spade,' she whispered, 'and a bottle of holy water.'

'What?' Paddy Joe was flummoxed.

'Go back to the field and bury it. Hide it quick! It was twins.'

It was so small he wouldn't have seen it from the headland only he knew where to look for it – a tiny thing all smeared with blood and slime and earth and dung, there in the drill. It was curled up like a dead sucker-pig; just as white, almost as small. Paddy Joe knew that it was dead, but he put a big hand on its breast to check – stone cold. Close to dread, he took one marble-sized knee between a forefinger and thumb and lifted the leg, thin as a pot-stick and already stiffening. Ah God-oh! Tch-tch-tch! Look at that! A grand wee *gasún*. Wasn't it a dread that the *girseach* hadn't been first out. What good was a *girseach* to a farmer? Still, God was good. He might send a son next year.

Paddy Joe took the bottle of well water from his pocket – there had been no chance to sneak holy water out past Eiley – and baptised the corpse. Just in case the soul still lingered. He thought of saying a prayer, but then thought better. If his baptism had been in time, the original sin had been washed away and the boy was in Heaven; if it hadn't, he was in Limbo, and could never see God's face. It was as simple as that. Paddy Joe remembered from his catechism that to waste a prayer for a soul beyond God's mercy was as grievous a sin as to doubt that mercy. A sin against hope. The one sin that could never be forgiven. He began to dig.

The hole was barely two feet deep when he heard a shout from the field gap. 'Aw, how a' ye, Ned?' He straightened, rested his two hands on the spade's haft, and stayed that way as long as he dared.

'The hard man!' Ned called, making his way along the headland. Casually, Paddy Joe toed the tiny corpse into the hole, and in the same way bent and spaded soil on top of it, and tramped it down. By the time his neighbour came close enough to stretch a hand, the infant, and all traces of its birth, were safely buried.

'Put it there,' Ned said. The two men shook. 'I hear you've the makings of a family at last,' Ned went on. Paddy Joe nodded. 'A *girseach?*'

'Aye.'

'Ah, well, sure – sure there's plenty more where she came from!' Ned threw back his goblin's head and roared with laughter. Paddy Joe smiled. 'Next year, please God,' Ned said, suddenly solemn.

'Please God,' Paddy Joe agreed.

'You're kept busy,' Ned remarked, after a pause.

'Aye. Plenty to do, some of us. It's brave weather,' Paddy Joe went on. 'Cowld, but good drying. I was just burying a stone. A big hoor that damn near put my shoulder out when I was opening the drills. I'm not the better of it yet.'

'Aw, big stones is a hoor,' Ned said seriously.

'Honest to God, every year I plough this field I hit it. Begod when I hit it yesterday I damn near fainted. I was no good for an hour. When I was coming back out there now, I seen the spade fornenst the pratie pit, and I sez to myself, I'll bury it.'

'Aw aye. Good job. Big stones is a hoor,' Ned said. 'They could strain the mandril of the plough. Or strain the horse. To say nothing of a Christian's shoulder.'

'Well, I'd better do another bit.'

Paddy Joe walked to the headland and planted the spade against the hedge. He watched Ned cast a disappointed look about the field. Not one snagging briar for the begrudging wee shibby-shite to crow about. The field was like a patch of brown corduroy stitched on the parish.

But: 'Christ Paddy Joe, that horse is shivering!' Ned said, shaking his head and sighing out of him. 'You should know better than to leave a sweatin' baste tied up in a cowld March wind. You might have foundered him.'

'Do you know what you might do, Ned. Next time you're passing, you might drop that saddle harrow back I lent you last year. I'll need to top these drills.'

'Aw God aye! To be sure, Paddy Joe, I'll do that. And I'll send Stephen over as soon as he gets home from school. Good luck, now.'

After Ned was gone, Paddy Joe stared over at his son's grave and, for just a moment, felt life wasn't fair: Ned with eight sons, him with none. But he dismissed his grief – it was bad luck to fret over what might have been far worse. It was like farming. Not to compare the Christian to the brute beast, but if you've livestock you'll have dead stock. He thanked God for His mercy. The girl would be a great help in the house, and there wasn't a bother on Maureen. She was good stock. They were only two years married, after all, and that wasn't too long, surely, for her to take to show something for his efforts. Even if it was a girl. Yes, he'd made a lucky match. Many another woman would have blabbed to that Barrett gabby-guts. They would have been destroyed. Next year, or the next, God might send a son. God was good. Hadn't He just proved it? Hadn't He spared them the shame of having somebody belonging to them in that weedy field behind the graveyard, the unconsecrated ground, where all the unbaptised were buried, suicides along with them?

Paddy Joe Fahy hitched the traces to the singletree, called to the horse, and split the ridges over his dead son.

Mad bastards

Big Mal thumbed one cartridge in with deliberation, then kissed the crudely sealed end of the other before offering it to the breech. It was a gesture that seemed oddly to heighten Liam's excitement and disquiet. Mal murmured something, a dedication or an appeal maybe, and smiled. He was cool, Big Mal, real cool. A mad bastard, but real cool.

It took a firm push to get the second cartridge home.

He'd been an expert at doctoring shotgun cartridges for almost half his life, Liam knew. Since he was twelve, Big Mal had been shooting feral goats in the Glens and on the Mournes and as close to Belfast as Cave Hill, even after the Troubles had broken out and it was a danger to be caught abroad with a gun – especially an unlicensed one. He shot them with half-inch steel ball bearings in place of lead pellets, sealed into the cartridge hull with melted candlewax, a slug that had the punch of a heavy-calibre rifle bullet at close range. Once, Mal had blown the entire lower jaw and muzzle off a big buck with such a slug. His last cartridge too – he'd had to finish the brute off with the gun butt.

The problem with the shotgun, he had explained to Liam, was its inaccuracy. Its unrifled bore meant it was necessary to get really close to be reasonably certain of hitting the target.

But sure that made for better sport!

'We'll let the bastard get to the near lamppost.' Mal's Northern drawl cut across Liam's thoughts, almost as if he'd read them. Liam was aware of this part of the plan. He nodded nervously.

Though of course there was no question of hitting the target this time. The cartridges were blank. Liam knew that. Big Mal had assured him. They'd been emptied of shot and resealed. They were only going to scare the guy.

Still, it was a serious matter to point a gun, loaded or not, never mind to discharge it at a man. Technically, legally, speaking, it was assault with a deadly weapon, and he, Liam, could be an accessory.

But they'd never be able to prove it. All he had to do was stick to the story. Mal had come to the Rooms and asked to crash out for a few hours. He'd gone into the bedroom – where they were now – and Liam had stayed in the living room revising for the exams. He'd assumed that Mal was sleeping. After the commotion Mal had just walked out and down the stairs. He'd walked, he hadn't run. Liam had been totally unaware of the devilment in his own bedroom.

It was a good story. It was just about credible, and it was in line with what the college authorities knew of Mal – what everyone knew about him. He was a mad bastard, but he had a knack of knowing how to time his exits with precision.

Like last night, in the Buttery bar, where they'd met as Big Mal had said in his letter they would. Mal had arrived in with the shotgun slung from the armhole of his trench coat by a meat hook through the trigger guard. He'd stood at the bar and let the coat swing open and the gun just be glimpsed, so that before they'd got the first pint sunk they'd had a wide if surreptitious audience. But while Liam was enjoying, as he always did, the attention Big Mal always attracted, Mal had murmured 'Let's go,' and as they were leaving by the back door they saw two porters hurrying down the front steps.

Or that other time, that famous time at the Hist debate on drugs. They'd sat at the back, Mal at the end of the row, next to the door, his chair thrown brazenly back on two legs, one foot on the other knee, nonchalantly gumming three Rizlas together and going through the procedure with unhurried care, seeming oblivious to the stares and silent excitement in their vicinity. He'd timed it so impeccably that he'd just lit up and blown a huge cloud of pungently unmistakable smoke towards the ceiling when that priest who'd spoken so passionately in the debate itself had answered a question from the floor, and assured the enquirer that marijuana was certainly not harmless.

Big Mal stood up then and interrupted. 'Well padre, I'm from the Northern Nonconformist tradition, and –' he took a deep draw, held it in his lungs for a moment, nodded at the No Smoking sign, and concluded through his intoxicating exhalation – 'I think you're full of shit.' He left then, while the place was still stunned into silence by his cheek, and he did it all so dismissively and carried it off so well that he deprived his opponent of the satisfaction of making an answer, yet gave no appearance of having run away. Case dismissed; next business. There had been quite a titter – even an attempt at applause. The priest had been furious, but one or two of his colleagues had had to hide their smiles. Mal was a mad bastard – but cool, real cool.

Of course the authorities thought he was a mad bastard too, and were only too glad to get rid of him. And he himself had presented them with the opportunity to do so. Imagine headbutting a lecturer across a Commons dinner table! Sometimes he could be daft as a brush.

Like now. Mad enough to bring a shotgun all the way from

Belfast across the border, and think nothing of it. 'It was wee buns, Liam, they never stop motorbikes.' And mad enough to aim and fire it at the man over whom he had already only narrowly escaped a charge of assault and battery, a man as bitter and stubborn as himself. And all over a harshly graded exam paper that only carried a few marks anyway. He was mad right enough. And so was Liam to be getting involved. The college might be anxious to avoid adverse publicity, but it might not be able to prevent the *gardaí* investigating a shooting, and possibly criminal prosecution. In Big Mal's case, it might not want to. Again Liam regretted agreeing to the proposal. Last night in the Pavilion bar it had seemed like great crack, after Mal had got him pissed and wound up. But now?

Big Mal chatted away about the job he was doing back home. Not a bother on him. It was good money, and the work wasn't too hard, and it was easy enough to skive off if he had a hangover. He mentioned that even if the college did kick up, he had an alibi: the time-clerk would have clocked him in that morning, and he'd be on the site by lunch time – as long as the old Bonneville held together at full throttle the whole way to Belfast. All Liam had to do was stick to the story. He'd seen nothing; he knew nothing. For his own part, Mal would simply deny everything.

But there might be witnesses who would say that Liam and Big Mal had been together in the Buttery and the Pavilion, and that Big Mal had had a gun inside his coat, and that he'd stayed overnight in Liam's rooms.

It was too late to welsh out now. Across Botany Bay, a familiar figure was ascending the steps from the Buttery, after religiously observed communion with mid-morning cup of coffee. That big head, that bush of red hair, that thrusting goat's beard were unmistakable.

'Here he comes,' Big Mal breathed, and took a sight down

the shotgun. He thumbed off the safety. He was cool, as cool as the blued steel that barely protruded beneath the sash. The twin muzzles were rock steady. 'Just let him get close enough to see the yellows of his eyes. Now if this was a twenty-two-two-fifty with a scope, I could blow the head off him from here.'

A tiny droplet of alarm trickled down Liam's spine. Those *are* blanks you've got in there? he wanted to be reassured. But it would be so uncool to ask.

O'Brien was halfway along the tennis courts. He was glancing at a quarter-folded copy of the *Irish Times* as he walked, as he did unless there was a hurry on him. The sound of bouncing balls and twanging catgut, calls and laughter, filled the air along with sunshine and the scent of blossom. It was, Liam thought, a peaceful scene – the thought struck him as inane.

It seemed to take a long time for O'Brien to cover the remaining distance.

'Tell you what, man,' Liam said softly. 'Just in case when he looks up he sees me with you, I'll go next door and watch from there. Okay?'

Big Mal nodded abstractedly. As he was turning away Liam spotted another familiar figure emerging from Number Seventeen: Wee Wilfie. Another Engineering guy. Another mad Northerner. Quiet-looking, softly spoken little fellow. Think butter wouldn't melt in his arse, as Big Mal said. But wild-out absolutely. Into everything except the crib at Christmas. And he'd be in that too, if he could ride the ass. They were all mad bastards, these Northerners.

He heard Big Mal say softly, 'Here we go,' and he hurried to the living room. By the time he reached the vantage point of the other window, O'Brien had passed the last lamppost but one, his tread heavy, his demeanour imperious as he walked with one eye on the paper, the other on the ground ahead. His rat-trap jaw and pugnacious pout were in half-profile. Wee Wilfie was abreast of him and overtaking, his thin hips articulating girlishly as he hurried as though to a lecture, late. A tattered folder and some books were clasped to his chest. His long lank hair was swinging below his fine-boned, artful face, his steel John Lennon glasses were slipped down on his narrow nose. There was that faint and famous smile about his lips, that innocent smile that had seduced a multitude.

Suddenly Wilfie looked up and for an instant his eyes met Liam's. His smile broadened, and Liam thought he might have winked. But he couldn't be certain because just then Wilfie turned as though towards the Engineering block – right below; right across O'Brien's path.

The shotgun blast reverberated round the walls. Silence descended on the courts. The sound of the traffic in Pearse Street became loud.

Wee Wilfie had dropped as though magically rendered boneless, so that O'Brien almost tripped over him. He lay there on the ground at the lecturer's feet, absolutely motionless, a tangle of thin torso and twisted limbs.

O'Brien stood there, looking stupidly down at him, obviously not understanding what had happened. The sound of the traffic grew faint in Liam's ears. He registered the rumble of window sashes, sensed rather than saw the eyes that stared. Then a girl screamed from the tennis courts – a single long piercing scream, followed by a series of short sharp shrieks.

'O'Brien,' Big Mal's voice followed.

The lecturer looked up. Liam saw deathly fear come into his eyes, raw terror etch itself into his face. His mouth was open. His eyes looked suddenly old. A driblet of saliva began to drool from his thick slack lower lip and got lost in the goatish wilderness. He took on the appearance of one who might die of fright there on the spot. He was such an awful-looking object that Liam almost felt sorry for him.

The girl kept shrieking. O'Brien kept staring upwards, like a rabbit fascinated by a stoat. A breeze ruffled the leaves of the newspaper on the ground, and scattered pages from Wee Wilfie's bursted folder.

'This one won't miss, O'Brien!' Big Mal shouted.

An animal whimper, so low that Liam thought he might only imagine he heard, escaped the lecturer's open throat. A dark stain spread rapidly down the legs of his grey suit. His body refused to move.

'You fucking coward!' Big Mal roared over the shrieks of the hysterical girl. 'You don't deserve it, but I'll give you a count of three. One –'

O'Brien leaped like a galvanised cadaver, spun around, and fled. The shotgun barked again. O'Brien screamed. The girl's shrieks ceased abruptly. On the periphery of his vision Liam saw her collapse. O'Brien kept screaming as he ran. The noise coming from next door sounded like a madman's laugh.

Liam turned from the window.

'Did you see it?' Mal had run in from the bedroom. He was still laughing crazily. 'Did you see? He pissed himself! He fucking pissed himself!'

'Get out!' Liam said. 'Get going quick! The porters'll be here in a minute.' There was an urgent rapping on the door.

'Relax man,' Big Mal said, cool as ever. 'They'll be shit-scared. They won't dare come in without the cops.'

'Pearse Street station's just across the road,' Liam snapped. The rapping was insistent. There was such a thing as being too cool. 'They're probably on their way already.'

'They won't hear it,' Mal said complacently. 'These high walls, the traffic –'

Liam turned the knob. The door burst open.

'Hey hey!' Big Mal beamed, and spread his arms wide, the heavy gun like a conductor's baton in his fingers. He clasped Wee Wilfie tightly. He kissed him resoundingly on both cheeks. 'Man, you were brill. Absolutely brill. Pity you couldn't have seen it. He fucking pissed himself. Ask Liam. He actually fucking pissed himself.'

'He actually fucking shit himself man!' Wee Wilfie shouted exultantly. 'I near stifled on the smell. It was rank.'

The pair of them danced around the room in an embrace, howling with manic laughter. Then Wee Wilfie broke off, looked at his watch, and said in O'Brien's Trinity accent: 'I've been getting drunk with three compatriots in the Harbour bar for the past two hours.' He snapped his fingers. 'Take me to my alibi!'

Liam urged them on fussily, all his anxiety returned.

'Lend us your brain-bucket,' Wee Wilfie said.

Liam fetched the crash helmet. 'Now get out, for Christ's sake.'

They vanished into wild whooping echoes on the stairwell. Within seconds Liam heard the rattle and the roaring of the Triumph, a squeal as it turned out of Side Gate, then an exultant bellow through its open pipes on Pearse Street before Big Mal dropped revs to catch second, and the buildings and the traffic swallowed it.

Liam was shaking. Now what would he do? They hadn't planned the thing in this detail. What should he do? Wait until the porters and the *gardaí* came? For a moment he thought of simply walking out and going to the library, pretending he'd been there all morning. But he could never make that stick. They'd break him down. They might even meet him on the stairs. He'd stick with Big Mal's story. But he wouldn't stay here. That would be un-cred – and totally uncool. He'd go to the porters' office at Front Gate and tell all that he was supposed to know, like an honest outraged straight would. He'd tell Big Mal all about it on the phone tonight. And wouldn't Big Mal laugh. He'd be real cool. He'd stick to the story. They wouldn't break him down.

On the tennis courts the girl who'd fainted was coming round. A small crowd of anxious-looking folk surrounded her. Liam hardly noticed. He was making up the details as he walked by.

THE LOANEN

PACKIE MAGUIRE SQUATTED IN A corner of the field away from the lane and hummed an air with uncommon violence. He reached into a pocket and took out the pouch of tobacco and papers, and rolled and gummed another cigarette and lit it. He didn't smoke as a rule, and the tobacco was dry and dusty since last he had been to a public bar, and he had neither ear nor liking for music; but he sucked on the skinny cigarette relentlessly, and coughed and hummed until his throat was sore. The tobacco would not stay lit, but that was no great drawback – the opposite, so long as his matches lasted. The heifer's time was up, and he knew that she was fretful and trying to settle, and to be able to stay quiet for her sake and to concentrate on the job in hand would have mightily pleased him.

But there were men beyond the hedge, waiting in the lane-way. Packie cursed under his breath. All day he'd been cursing softly, with no real spleen, but by now his wry patience and good humour were deserting him. Men behind hedges were not to be laughed at. Not after dark. Not in south Armagh.

At first he'd assumed that a routine British Army patrol had stumbled upon him, so he coughed and struck up a match and a tune to advertise his presence, and prepared answers to questions that might be put to him. If he was challenged he had nothing to hide. He was an honest man, a farmer who could not choose his working hours or tell his heifers when to calve. He knew Marty Murtagh to be sure – wasn't he a neighbour? – but only to say hello to. He hadn't seen the man in years, and didn't care if he never saw him again, as long as he kept his eyesight.

Then he recalled that there had been only a distant hum of helicopters in all the hours since he'd left home. Which suggested that it might be the Provos who had something in the wind. Especially as there had been activity about Murtagh's old place.

But it could always be the SAS. The Special Air Services did none of the things expected of ordinary British soldiers. Not for them the decent warning of a helicopter descending in a roaring swirl of wind and dust, belching frightened squaddies from its belly. No. Them lads could lie out like bullocks till their horns grew into their eyes, catch rabbits better than a lurcher could, and eat stones to sharpen their teeth. And like rogue dogs after sheep, you never knew where they'd turn up.

But whoever was lurking in the laneway, soldiers or IRA men, Packie was too close for comfort, and could not get away. His lips twitched as he cursed the Provos and the army, the heifer for coming to her time just now, and the rig bull for serving her nine months before. Then he cursed his own carelessness for not having properly dressed that calf, and for not having brought the heifer back to the home farm when he'd known her time was near. But he'd been busy with the harvest, and had assumed or hoped she wouldn't calve till it was saved. He'd hardly thought it necessary to bring the flashlight and the rope, and had felt almost foolish at his preparations. He'd even brought an egg.

★

His day's misfortunes had begun when the van broke down, a victim of good intentions. The clutch had been slipping for a week, and that trailerload of pigs had finally nailed it yesterday. He'd had to trudge across the shoulder of the mountain to the outfarm on the Ballinoga back road, and Packie was slow with age, and soft with plastic van seats now. And of course, when you're down, down with you: the breakdown had caused knock-on delays, so that the evening was well advanced by the time he got away, taking to the fields and then to the heather, until the rocky upper reaches of Caipin Dubh's lane began to lead his steps downhill and give his legs and lungs a break.

Then, as his bad luck would further have it, he fell in with Poet O'Callaghan, pushing his bicycle and singing like a demented thrush. Packie raised a martyr's eyes to heaven, and resigned himself to putting up with long-worded windy nonsense for the remainder of the trek to the road.

Not that the Poet was anything but a harmless eejit. To be sure he could pass for a lunatic any time he liked, but he was civil. A smart fellow too – a mass o' brains. He'd been on television once, and spoken very well, and though it had been double Dutch to Packie, the audience had clapped, and there had been professors and a bishop and all classes of clever men and women there.

But for all the good the brains did him, the Poet's head might as well be full of mad dog's shite. Personally, Packie was convinced that he had too much brains – which could be just as bad as not enough. Who but an *amadán* would live in that forlorn shanty on Slieve Bracken, with neither chick nor child to share it, when he could have a nice wee Housing Executive cottage in the town? And of course the drink was a curse on the poor fellow too. He'd been in and out of dry dock in Saint Luke's for years. He was more to be pitied than laughed at.

The Poet said he was going to Castleglen.

'Heading in for the few pints, Poet?' Packie said agreeably. You'd swear he'd asked if he was going in to rob the wine from off the altar. The Poet stopped so suddenly he all but fell over his bike, and threw the two hands up at the sky in horror.

'Perish the thought, Packie! Never, never, never again! After the last skite I vowed against the loathsome stuff, and may the gods forsake me if I be forsworn.' The eyes rolling and the hands going good-o the whole time, as though the flies were at him, long bony fingers raking through the wild grey hair as he described some of the sufferings he'd gone through. The passion and death of Our Lord could hardly match them.

'Oh no, no, no, no, no! I have indeed set my steps towards an alehouse, Packie, but there I shall have nothing stronger than Ballygowan.' Whatever that might be. 'The Committee has asked me to give a reading as part of the south Armagh festival.'

'Oh?' Packie stole a glance at his companion. A quare-looking tulip, wouldn't you think, to be going anywhere except a circus. All he was short of was the greasepaint. The head was like a hoar-frosted whin bush, he hadn't stood very close to the razor, and the rigout he was decked in would put you in mind of a flag on a short staff. If you met him on the street you'd give him a penny.

'Oh,' Packie said again. 'That's, ah – that's very good, Poet.'

You couldn't even talk about the weather to the Poet, like you would to a normal Christian. But Packie did his gallant best.

'Grand spell o' weather, Poet.'

'I quite agree, Packie. The gods are well-disposed. We must give thanks to the Higher Power that sustains us all when the harvest's home.'

Wouldn't you think by the crack he had a field full of gods

to keep great with? He must be some class of a Protestant now. Packie didn't know a great deal about Protestants, beyond that they didn't believe in the One True God, and had harvest thanksgivings in September, and said that Our Lady was a prostitute and Christ himself a bastard – God forgive them. And that was enough for Packie. Civil enough craythurs, mind, the few of them he knew, and he said the odd prayer for their conversion. But a man could never trust them.

He cast another sideways glance at the Poet and tried again. 'Another good day the morrah' – nodding westward.

That really wound the Poet up. He went on and on about the colours and the shadows and reflections, and the miracle the sunset was, and how privileged they were to see it. Privileged, note. A miracle, no less! As if the same sun hadn't been rising and setting every day since God was a *gasún*.

'Right enough, it's lovely,' Packie agreed, glancing towards the spectacle above the Cavan hills. The Poet didn't seem to hear. He actually stopped the bicycle and stood to watch the last rays die. Stood for ages. Struck dumb of a sudden. Only, Packie thought, that he himself had been well brought up, he would have walked on and left him there, standing like a stray cock at a christening. Eventually the Poet fell into step, but he looked so woebegone that Packie felt obliged to cheer him up.

'Sure you'll see it again the morrah, Poet.'

By the look he got, you'd think that it was *his* head was cut.

That was almost all of Packie's contribution to the bewildering bullshit that passed for conversation. The Poet could keep crack with a haggard of sparrows, and was supposed to be powerful value with a few drinks in him; but sober he'd put years on a banshee. The constant chatter and the enormous words got on Packie's nerves. He grabbed his chance when they passed the only other house along the lane and saw the open door.

'Is your neighbour home, Poet?' – with heavy irony.

Marty Murtagh or Man-Killer Murtagh – depending on your sympathies – hadn't haunted south Armagh in years; but it was known that his house was used for unquestioned purposes from time to time. After breaking out of Long Kesh a few years back, adding two more lives to a lengthy list, Murtagh had lived for some time around Dundalk. Later, after the SAS began cross-border raids, he'd fled farther south. Since then he'd fallen foul of the Irish security forces – and of his old companions, whose own shenanigans were upset by his maverick recklessness and the flurries of security forces that followed him and his small band of paramilitary renegades. He lived on the run the whole time now, snatching a night's sleep here and a day's rest there, with whomever there was left who would shelter him.

'I know little, Packie, and I care less!' The genteel accent slipped a little under the weight of contempt. The Poet was no lover of men of violence, and made no secret of the fact. He'd written a poem once, 'Two of a Kind', about an SAS man and a Provo, spitted head to head over the same fire in Hell. It was a powerful poem. Packie had heard it. An English singer, with long hair and a beard on him, had put it to music and made a record; but it had pleased nobody. After a radio station that played it was bombed a couple of months back, that was the end of it. A great pity. It might have made poor Poet a bit of money.

And that finished Packie's attempt to escape from the daftest oul codology about – whatever it was that the Poet was going on about: dust and volcanoes and stars, and things that had happened back in Oul God's day, with the Poet blathering on as if he'd been around at the time and seen it all with his own two eyes.

'Probably the sister in,' Packie supposed. Saoirse Murtagh

maintained the house, she said, against the day that her brother would be free to walk his own land without fear of the ancient enemy or of traitors and collaborators.

But there was no car at the road.

It was a good thing, after all, that he had come prepared. The bones had slipped the whole way, and he wasn't two hours in the field when the heifer put out the bag. Packie investigated with hard, tough, gentle hands. Through the membrane he could feel the jellied hoofs and, behind, the muzzle with the tongue inside the mouth. So far so very good. But they could still have quite a way to go.

Time, like the calf, moved slowly. Restlessly the heifer roved, seeking sometimes the shelter of the hedges, other times the exposure of the field. Thus the last of the twilight's afterglow gave way to darkness, and Packie waited, and heard the stealthy movements of the watchers in the lane, and began to smoke and hum, and to rehearse his answers.

The night was dark, the field as lonely as the stars – the stars the Poet imagined he'd seen born. There was no other light in the mountain fold. It was a lonely old life he led, Packie thought. It would be nice, at such a time as this, to have a strapping big son to wait up with a sick beast, or a small grandson to keep him company, a child at whose fear of the darkness or of bogeymen an old man might chuckle and, chuckling, shed his own fear of skulking watchers on the far side of a hedge.

But regrets for what might have been, memories of Mary, Anne and Lucy, all now grandmothers of other men's grandsons, were a waste of time. Desire, like the seed of the parable, had been spilled on barren ground. Packie felt a surge of shame and guilt. But it was all the will o' God – if it wasn't a sin to think so. And who could understand that? And who was he to be rearing up against it? God would understand. And even if He couldn't, He would still forgive.

Packie took out his beads and said the full fifteen decades of the rosary. For forgiveness for the sins of his youth and of his angry middle age. And for the souls of the dead: his ma and da, his brother and two sisters, and all who had gone before. And for all who had no one to remember them, to shorten their stint in Purgatory. Praying was as good a way to pass the time as any. He might be in the field till dawn and after it, because the half-castrated rig had been a Charolais cross, and Charolais throw big calves, and the heifer was an undersized yearling. He said the last decade for the poor wee craythur, that she wouldn't suffer too much hardship.

Eventually her labour slowed the heifer down, though for long she fought off settling. Even when she did she could not seem to decide whether it was better to stand hump-backed with extended tail, or lie down stiff-legged and awkward. After the bag burst Packie investigated again. He was pleased enough by her progress, though he wished she had settled somewhere else. She had chosen the shelter of the hedge that marched along the lane, behind which he had heard the watchers. Packie listened again now. His matches were gone but the flashlight batteries were holding out. The troubled panting of the heifer and the beating of his own heart seemed to be the only sounds. He held his breath. No stir of life came from the lane. He let the breath out in gusty relief. The watchers must be gone.

There was a thump as the heifer dropped to the ground; then a weary, almost Christian groan. An outstretching hoof sliced the thin turf. Packie switched on the flashlight and approached her from the rear. He heard her grunt, saw her convulse. With surprising suddenness, two tiny shiny hoofs sprouted like wet buds from her.

The heifer groaned again and laboured. Packie dropped the light and took a rope from his pocket, got onto his knees and slipped a loop around each foot, reaching inside the passage to place it high up on the foreleg. He tightened the loops carefully, took up the slack, and waited for the animal to push again.

An alien sound intruded. Mumbled conversation from the road. No: a single voice – singing – drunk.

'Take me for a night in Dundalk ...'

A send-up of a song heard on the wireless. Packie nodded cynically. God help Head-o'-wit! The Poet had broken out again. Though come to think of it, it didn't sound like Poet. The voice was a thick, slurred, south Armagh brogue, and the singer was on foot, with no clicking freewheel to betray a supporting bicycle.

Surely it could never be – ? No, Murtagh couldn't be staying at home – could he? Or if he was, he wouldn't be such a fool as to get drunk – would he? And he'd never be alone – surely? When the singing stopped, Packie strained to hear sounds from the lane. There were none. If it was Murtagh, he could be the luckiest man in the country.

Unless of course, the watchers had been friends of his ...

'Take me for a night in Dundalk,

Take me for a night in Dundalk ...'

The voice was striking up again. It was closer now, almost at the foot of the lane. Suddenly it broke off in a mad howl.

'Take me drunk, I'm home!' The heifer flinched. The singer roared hilariously. 'Take me drunk – I'm home, I tell ye! Somebody take me drunk. Somebody, take me. Take me!' The heifer flinched again.

I'll take you by the throat if I lay hands on you, you unmannerly cur, whoever you are. Aloud, Packie soothed the heifer. 'Suck-suck-suck-suck. Poor wee pet.' It mightn't be

Murtagh at all. It might be someone else entirely. Someone who lived farther along the road.

But for the life of him, Packie couldn't imagine who that might be.

The calf was doing nicely. The head had been born. It was going as well as Packie could hope. The drunk lapsed into silence, and quickly receded from Packie's awareness, and whether he was the Poet or the Provo or another ceased to matter. Packie tensed with the heifer and pulled as she pushed, and half a yard of new life slid into the world. It balked at the loins.

A good pull now could finish it. But the kidneys could be a tricky spot too. Packie waited, tense, but patient. At the end it was down to God and nature. All Packie could do was his best when the time came.

He heard the dull, heavy sound as of a body falling. It came from the laneway. Was it Murtagh or the Poet? A mumbled curse; a shout, from only a few yards away.

'Divil shoot ye for a moon! If it was a bright night you'd be there!' And then the bray of a lunatic laugh.

God's curse on you and the moon! Would you ever shut up? But the heifer seemed to be beyond distraction now. She bawled in agony and uncomprehending fear, her head twisted round to look at the man and what was happening to her. In the misdirected beam of the flashlamp lying on the ground, the whites of her eyes were wide enough to back a waistcoat. Packie heard the voice: low, slurred, indistinct. Whose was it? What was he saying?

The heifer shuddered, clamoured. Packie heaved on the rope, and the calf seemed to move a little. But the contraction quickly passed, and the heifer drooped in exhaustion.

An unaccountable worry took hold of Packie then. Something wasn't right. He checked the calf. It was alive – as he had known it was. Might it be that he was about to lose the heifer? Surely not. She'd had an easier time of it than she had any right to expect. She'd lost little strength or blood. Surely she wasn't going to die on him at this stage?

But a lifetime of daily communion with the earth insisted that something was terribly, terribly wrong.

Suddenly there was a deafening report – close at hand – beside him! Packie gasped. The heifer started, tried to scramble to her feet – in vain. She bawled again, her bass note rising to a thin high pitch of panic. Her body convulsed. Packie, as terrified as she, but only slightly less captive to her confinement, threw his weight against the rope. There was another gunshot. No short, sharp little crack of a twenty-two, or the dry wicked rattle of machinegun-fire, heard in local skirmishes from time to time. This was the devastating, ear-splitting anger of a shotgun. Packie shouted in horror, called in frenzied aspiration on the Mother of God. The heifer almost screamed. Her hoofs scrabbled on the turf. Something gave. Packie lost his footing. His heels skidded on the greasy grass behind her, but his hands held fast to the slimy rope, and as he tumbled backwards there was a warm wet sluice and the calf was born.

The shotgun thundered again.

He pressed himself flat to the ground. He reached for the lamp and switched it off. He raised himself enough to feel for the muzzle of the calf in the darkness, and wiped the mucus from its mouth. He waited with a different sort of anxiety until he heard it breathe.

Packie Maguire sank back onto the ground, trembling. The heifer rested for a moment too, then clambered to her feet. She turned to nuzzle the strange wet silent hardly moving thing between her and the man. The calf, still dazed by its birth, slowly raised its head. It moaned. The heifer replied. She lost her hesitancy, licked her calf.

Packie began to recover, though still he trembled, still he prayed, silently now, to Our Lady and Her Son, to deliver him from evil this night.

But a lifetime's habits and generations of hunger asserted themselves. He fumbled in his pockets for the raw egg and the oatmeal. He'd cushioned the egg in newspaper, but it had smashed. He shredded the soggy insulation, and scooped the shelly mess into one hand as best he could, and wiped the pulp into the calf's mouth and closed it, massaged the gullet till he felt it move. He scattered the oatmeal over the damp body – though the heifer was in no need of encouragement.

'Good wee craythur' – almost aloud.

Only then did he approach the hedge. Furtively, fearfully; the flashlamp in one hand, unlit. There had been no sounds after the third gunshot, but when he was close to the hedge and silent, he could hear phlegmatic, ragged gasping, and he knew that somebody was dying.

And suddenly an awful thought struck Packie. An awful dread. An awful responsibility. An awful thought that overcame his terror. Somebody was dying – unshriven. Going to meet his Maker in a state of mortal sin.

Packie ran to the gateway and along the road, the flashlamp beam zigzagging on the mossy tarmac. He slowed a bit when he came to the lane, but out of concern for its broken surface and his own joints rather than fear of anything he might find in it, and he quickened his pace when the beam picked out the prone form on the ground.

Rage fought with pity for a place in Packie's heart then. The poor unfortunate harmless fool! God damn the bloody bastards! The silver hair, what was left of it, had told him who the victim was, but that would not have mattered. He would do the same for the local murderer, or a stranger in a foreign uniform. They were all somebody's rearing, all children of God, all entitled to enter God's glory if they repented at the end and made their peace. Incredibly, breath still rattled in the throat, gory froth still bubbled in the nostrils – but a glance was enough to tell that the body was destroyed beyond all hope of salvage. All that remained was the soul.

He tore the rosary beads out of their purse and dropped onto his knees. With ungentle urgency he grasped and raised the shattered ruin of a head. The stench of scorched hair and brains and cordite was enough to make him retch, but he swallowed back his gorge. He pressed the image of the slaughtered Saviour to the slack red lips of the dying man, and thought back to his school days, and what the catechism said any lay confessor had to do. He chanted all that he remembered.

'Oh my God, I am heartily sorry for having offended Thee, and I detest my sins above every other evil . . .'

Of the killers not a sign remained.

A WORLD FULL OF PLACES

HE HAD LIZZIE-ANN FLAT on her back under the inky ivy bush, hidden by the haystacks from the house. And Lizzie-Ann's legs were up in the air and pointing at opposite hedges. And the world was warm and bright, and black and white, with a full moon in the sky. And he had one arm to the shoulder up Lizzie-Ann's skirt, holding a bunched fistful of her drawers. And the most beautiful thing about it was the way the black moon looked, reflected in her eyes, shining with joy. And he'd ripped off her drawers and rolled her over, and was about to mount her like the stallion mounts the mare, when a bony knee hit him on the hip, and the old fellow growled in his ear.

'Come on, Teddy. Get up, Teddy. Up ye get. Don't have me calling you again. Don't have us waking the women.'

Teddy opened his eyes, groggy with sleep and disappointed lust. In the far corner of the murky room, he could make out the other bed and the humped shapes of his wife and her mother beneath the coats and blankets. He could hear them snoring.

Teddy hauled himself out of the bed he shared with his father-in-law. He sat on the side of it with his feet on the packed-earth floor, and scratched himself through his singlet, and waited for the bone in his drawers to soften. No use running to the byre or the barn to get rid of it this morning: Old Dan would be after him, scalding him to get him started.

'We'll get you on the road early,' Dan whispered in the kitchen. 'Get her home and tried out before dark. Open a few drills, with the help o' God, and sow some mangolds.'

Teddy said nothing.

'Run out like a good chap and drive the cows in,' Dan said softly. 'Save Lizzie-Ann. Troth it's her'll be the busy girl this day.' He raked back the *gríosach*, placed a few turf sods on the fire, and began to turn the fan bellows. 'I'll get the stirabout ready.'

There was a trail of mist along the river, though it was only August. It thickened downstream. Beneath it in the distance, Dundalk Bay looked like a white sea. Beyond Slieve Gullion the sun was stretching and yawning. As he climbed the hill he felt the faint warmth of its rays on the back of his neck. In the rushy hollow beyond, the two cows stirred at his call, but he had to go up to them as always and clap a hand on the dewy hide of one before they rose. They ambled towards the house, and the calves and yearlings followed, the horse behind.

A thin blue haze of smoke was standing straight up from the chimney. In the kitchen the two women were at the table, and Dan was spooning porridge into four bowls. Biddy smiled slyly at her son-in-law; Lizzie-Ann didn't look at him. They breakfasted in silence, apart from Dan blathering about the new plough, and about the great man Teddy was to have about the place.

After he caught and harnessed the horse, Teddy slung a steel slide – to protect the sole-plate of the plough on the road home – from one point of the hames, a singletree from the other, and hooked the ends of the trace chains to the backrope. Biddy sprinkled holy water over him and the horse, and called on

God to bring them home safely with the plough. 'Don't forget – you're meeting Lizzie-Ann after to get the seed,' she shrilled. Teddy said nothing. Lizzie-Ann was going out to milk as he set off down the lane, her big belly away from him, her hefty bottom towards him. It hadn't looked like that last night, he thought. At the road he brought the Clydesdale to the verging bank and clambered up. He seated himself far back towards the horse's rump, and clicked against his teeth.

That's not the way to sit a horse, cobber! He could hear his Uncle Con's voice, deep and hearty as it had been when Con had come home. *Sit forward, on his back, not on his arse! Take control of him. Show him who's boss.*

Uncle Con had ridden horses – half-wild 'brumbies' he'd called them – in Australia, herding sheep and cattle. He boasted that he'd never found the horse he couldn't master. But he'd had a saddle, with stirrups for his feet, Teddy thought irritably, not a ridge of bone to sit on. He'd killed horses, Uncle Con had. Walked one into the ground across the Gibson Desert, and almost died himself before he'd crawled to water. Shot a few. Battered more to death for reasons Teddy couldn't fathom. Much of Uncle Con's manhood was a mystery, even much of what he told in tales like these.

Uncle Con was reedy-voiced and feeble now, but he was still alive, four years after he'd come home to die, with nothing to show for a lifetime but a few dust-catchers: a boomerang; a broken shield; a shrunken heathen's head which soon stank in the damp Irish air. Teddy's mother threw it in the fire one day. When he found out, Uncle Con just laughed. 'In the flames like his pagan soul! The hairy bastard'll get even with me yet.'

He laughed too at the Devlins – 'Misery riding on Poverty's back!' – and he laughed at his nephew when he heard that Teddy was marrying Lizzie-Ann. At least, at first he laughed.

'What you doing that for, cobber, hey? Whelp of a she-dingo and a poor oul eejit with no more balls than a bullock. You do that and you'll end the same. Sleeping on a hayloft or in a settlebed if you're lucky, asking your wife's say-so to have a piss or chalk your wire.'

Teddy had been awed and thrilled by his uncle's irreverence, amazed by his mother's tolerance of such language in the house. She wouldn't have taken it from Teddy's father, Lord rest his soul.

'What you want to get married to that one for, hey? The land? Hah! Much good that did Dan Devlin. All you need of land is six feet, cobber, and I knew good men whose bones were never buried. Shark shit in the China Sea, or rolling round the Nullarbor. You could do better. You're no oil painting, no more than myself, but that young one has a face like a kangaroo's arse, and an arse you'd hang a britchin on. I rode better-looking darkies.' It was just after the bans were to be read, and Uncle Con had long stopped laughing.

As always when he thought of Uncle Con now, Teddy got defensive – of both his uncle and himself – and confused. His ma was right. Con was a drunken bousie who'd got a girl in trouble back in the 1860s and run away to sea. Her father had put the girl out on the road, and her brother had opened Uncle Con's head with an ashplant half a century later. Caught him outside McCreesh's shop before he was a week back in the country. But Uncle Con was a holy terror! With blood in his eyes, he got up off his back, fighting. He'd come home to die, but he wasn't dead yet – no, not by a long shot. He pulled the stick off the other old man, and laid into him with his fists, and cracked between his toothless jaws the thumb of one of the younger men who tried to haul him off, and flattened the nose of another. Four of them were pumping blood before they got him rasselled to the ground.

Jaysus, Uncle Con was a holy dread!

Teddy couldn't look Uncle Con in the face any more. At the wedding he'd dragged Teddy to one side. He was well gone in drink, and you couldn't stop him talking.

'*Gasún a mhic*, will you take an oul fool's advice and get out while there's still time. Give her the slip tonight, after you do the job. Hide in a coalboat on the docks, same as I did. You'll be in Liverpool tomorrow. But get out with your two stones while you have them, or that cuddy'll cut you, sure as you cut boar pigs with a blade. You'll be like her oul fellow, sleeping on a hay-bed in the loft like a hiring-boy.'

Rolling with the Clydesdale's heavy gait, Teddy thought glumly that perhaps his uncle had been right. If this was married life it wasn't much: dreaming of a lassie's backside in a bed beside her da, and chalking your wire in the byre.

The sun was warm on his face. He put his hands onto the hairy broad back and humped forward. He settled himself behind the backrope, and kicked with his hobnailed heels.

'Come up! Come up, ye hoor ye!' The Clydesdale whiffled and trotted a few clumsy steps. Teddy's teeth rattled, and his tailbone hammered on the knobby ridge of spine. The horse resumed its walk, and Teddy slithery-arsed back onto the fleshy pad above the loins.

'Hey!' Teddy started and almost tumbled off; he hadn't heard the bicycle. Lizzie-Ann pulled up beside him. 'Don't forget, now,' she warned. 'I'll see you outside Saint Nicholas's at twelve o'clock. If I'm not there wait for me. Don't try to get that mangold seed on your own. Them fellas would see you coming, and try to sell you bicycle seed, and you'd be bawkie enough to buy it.' Teddy nodded. 'And hey,' she added. 'In front of the chapel, you gam. Not behind it.'

Teddy nodded again. His wife pedalled away, her big bottom shifting on the saddle, two bulging bags of eggs, packed in straw, dangling from the handlebars, the basket tied on the carrier behind.

The first of the guinea-hunters met him almost two miles from Lisdoo, a stranger in a faded hacking jacket, with a threadbare sandy moustache worked into thin waxed points.

'Hey hey!' the guinea-man began. 'A promising animal, what? A little rough, and past his prime like myself, but with potential.' A thick Newry accent made his chat sound silly and sad. 'Worth a tenner in normal times, old chap, but in these strange days we have to live in, I'll offer you hundred per cent. Twenty pounds. You won't do better.'

Teddy was puzzled. If a guinea-man was opening with twenty pounds on the high road, for the few shillings of a cut he'd get out of it, what were the big dealers closing with on the fairgreen?

'Twenty pounds?' he said, wondering if he'd heard right.

'Ah, don't be misled by outlandish rumour, my young friend,' the man said gravely. 'Twenty pounds is a very good price for such a sorry beast as this.'

'I'm not selling. I'm just going to pick up a plough.' Teddy nodded at the ploughslide hanging from the hames.

The seedy-looking stranger sighed. 'My sorrow. What the Kaiser's brought the world to. I'll probably cut my throat tomorrow, but I'll go twenty-two.'

'He's not for sale.'

'You would be wise to change your mind.'

'He's not my horse.' Teddy clicked and tossed the reins.

'You'll never get a better price. Not for this faded yeoman,' the man called after him in chirpy warning. 'Prices have fallen back already, I'm reliably informed. It's just a flash in the pan really. It'll all be over by Christmas.'

Within half a mile another stopped him, and was still blathering alongside, scalding him, when Teddy saw a third, haggling at Lisdoo Cross with a man who had passed him earlier, on a bicycle, leading two high-stepping Irish Draught colts. The colts, it struck Teddy as he passed, were gingered-up for a sale: they looked too frisky for their rib-slatted, sweat-lathered hides.

Dundalk was packed even for a fair day. Teddy slid off the Clydesdale's back and tied the reins to the handles of a turnip barrow in front of the hardware shop. The Bummer McCoy, who'd lost his two legs in the Boer War, was there on his little wheeled tray, beating his two wooden blocks in time to his chant. 'Help Lord Kitchener! A penny for Lord Kitchener!' The mind was gone as well. It was barely nine o'clock, but inside the shop Bellingham Barney already had an oily sheen on his forehead. Teddy had to wait a long time in the dusty shadows before speaking to him.

'Ah yes, Dan Devlin's man.' A hired man, Teddy thought with sudden resentment – that's how he was regarded. 'Come in here.' The shopkeeper led the way into a pokey office.

'Look,' he said, his pencil working, 'take this back to Syl in the yard – you know Syl? He'll know what to do.' He tore off a chit and handed it to Teddy. Teddy turned to go.

'Oh, and here.' The shopkeeper dug into an apron pocket. He reached out a hand. 'Take this.' He dropped two half-crowns into Teddy's palm. 'The penny back for luck,' he explained. 'I let Dan go the other day without it.'

He must have registered Teddy's look, for he chortled.

'It's good times for Ireland at last! We can all afford the luck-penny now.'

'Good times?' Teddy was more puzzled than ever. It was quare times anyway if Bellingham Barney was giving money away. Softest part of Barney was his teeth. Take surgery to get a shilling out of him. A dry-land pirate Uncle Con called him. Old Dan had grumbled that not one penny of good luck had he given back with the plough. Biddy had jeered at her husband and said he was no man.

'Of course. Good times for us all. We're at war, my lad! The Kaiser's at war with the King. First cousins falling out!' His mutton-chop whiskers spread for a moment in a busy man's laugh. 'There's army buyers on the fairgreen. Horses going for a hundred pounds, I hear. Old nags fit for the knacker going for half that. You ought to try that fellow out there. It'll all be over by Christmas, you could buy another cheap then. Mention it to Dan. Say I told you.'

He pushed Teddy out and closed the office door. 'What goes round comes round – the luck, you know?' He added a bit severely: 'Be sure to give that quarter-sovereign on to Dan, now.'

Teddy said nothing. It was his money that had paid for the plough.

He stepped into the sunlight of the street, the two coins heavy on his thigh. He realised that in the five months since his marriage this was the first time he had money in his pocket – he who'd had the name of being lucky with money. When he'd been hiring he'd always got generous masters, and in the year he'd been a free man, working about the farm at home with his brother, he'd seldom gone long without a turn from saving hay or turf, or road mending, or a day here and there in the forge. He was a good hard worker, as Uncle Con said, he didn't drink or smoke, and he knew that it was for all these things that Biddy had allowed a younger son with brothers at home to court her daughter, a girl with thirteen acres coming with her.

All these things, if not another thing. But Teddy didn't want to think about that possibility. He'd made his bed; he'd have to lie on it – whoever might have lain on it before him.

He reached for the reins, then paused and stared after a

familiar-looking arse he'd spotted dodging into Bachelors Walk. He left the Clydesdale tied to the turnip barrow, and walked to the corner. He saw the old arse lurch along the street and turn into a doorway. He followed.

The smell of beer and sawdust was unfamiliar but, in a queer way, remembered and welcoming – like the face of a childhood friend on the threshold: a friend he'd forgotten. Early though it was, there were a half-dozen men in the public bar, haggling or sealing deals, spitting on palms and slapping or holding back. The old man was at the bar, a glass of whiskey in his hand. Teddy came up behind, the sawdust muffling his hobnails. He heard a little moan of pleasure, a smack of lips. He clapped his hand down hard on the old man's shoulder.

'Aha, y'oul' bousie, I caught you.'

'God blast ye!' Uncle Con whirled on his stool. He laughed then. 'Teddy, *a mhic*. I thought it was that snakey brother of yours.' He reached out and took his nephew by the wrist and pulled him close. 'I gave her the slip.' His cloudy old eyes were twinkling. 'Your ma. Quigley was taking a cartload of pigs in, and he gave me a lift on the shaft.'

Teddy laughed at the deceit.

'You'll have a drink,' Con said. 'You will, you will! You're a man now. Wedded and bedded now.'

For just a moment Teddy hesitated. Aye, wedded and bedded – bedded with an oul man. Much good was it doing him!

'Begod I will!'

'Good man, good man. Hey boy!' Con bawled.

'But I'll get it myself,' Teddy said, remembering the quarter-sovereign in his pocket. He knew that his mother collected Con's old age pension herself, and that Con couldn't have more than a few coppers on him.

'Well?'

Before the dark-eyed stare of the white-shirted barman, Teddy fidgeted and flushed. His uncle had forced whiskey on him at his wedding breakfast, but it had turned his stomach, and his mother always called it lunatic soup.

'Well?' the severe pale face with its severe black moustache insisted.

'A . . . porter.'

'Pint?'

'Eh . . . aye.'

'One pint o' loose porter.'

Teddy nodded. The barman had already turned away. He tossed a big glass high in a gleaming spinning arc and caught it in the other hand behind his back. Teddy stared. The barman smirked. He pumped the glass full, topped it off with froth out of an enamelled jug, and set it on the bar.

'And a whiskey,' Teddy added. The barman brought it. He frowned at the thick white coin.

'Think this is the Bank of England? You'll have to wait for your change. It's not ten o'clock yet.'

Teddy sucked the bitter black liquid through the thick white froth, trying not to make a face. Beside him Con cackled. The barman curled his lip.

'Beat it down ye, cobber. Once you get the tooth for it you'll never get enough of it. God bless you,' Con added, taking the whiskey from Teddy and pouring it into his own.

For a short while they were silent. The barman was close at hand, making out to be polishing a glass, but with a smirk on him. Unmannerly class of a bastard.

'We'll sit down there,' Teddy said. Con followed to a corner, then went out the back. Teddy sat at the low table and sipped at his porter, and thought about his wife and last night's dream. It was to this town they had been brought after their wedding, old Dan driving the borrowed trap, drunk for once but talking shite as always, Teddy trying to catch hold of Lizzie-Ann's hand beneath the goatskin rug. Here they'd had their day in town and their night in bed. And a poor enough day it had been, and a poorer night. He thought gloomily of his uncle's scorned advice as the porter settled in his belly. Aye, a damn poor day. And a miserable night. And in the five months since he hadn't got his hand up Lizzie-Ann's skirt as many times, and hadn't done the stallion-on-the-mare job more than twice.

'What time is it?' he asked a man going out the back. The man pointed at the clock behind the bar and left. 'Eh . . . what time is it?' Teddy asked the barman. The barman turned and looked at the clock and drawled, 'Just gone half-ten.'

Teddy scowled at the smirk but held his tongue. An hour and a half before he had to meet Lizzie-Ann.

Con returned and sat down. 'How come you're in town?' Teddy explained. 'Bejaysus Dan Devlin's coming up rightly in the world,' Con sneered, 'if he can buy a plough!' Teddy said nothing. His uncle grasped his arm. 'Or is that the way of it, *a mhic*? Is that she-dingo spending your money for you?'

Teddy said nothing.

'Christ, *gasún* . . .' Con said. 'I hear you put a hill on her – the young one,' after a sip, he went on, then peered cutely.

It was a question. Teddy flushed. 'I think so,' he muttered. He could feel his uncle's gaze on him. He swallowed a big mouthful of porter.

'Are you sure,' Con said, his eyelids narrowed, 'there wasn't a cuckoo in the nest before you?'

Teddy felt the hairs walking on his head with shame.

'Ah Christ, *gasún!*' Con groaned. He shook his head. 'And I told you! I knew the seed and breed of her. No badness on poor oul Devlin's side, but there was never a Butler that was any good. No more in my time than in yours.'

'Hey!' Teddy called. The barman looked over. 'Eh ... the same again.'

Con paid; Teddy let him.

'If only you'd listened to me,' Con said sorrowfully as they supped. His hand was on Teddy's elbow. 'If only you'd listened. You should have just took her, the way the rooster takes the hens. Pin her to the ground and ride her, that's the way. That way you would have gone in on your own terms, not on that oul she-dingo's.' A sour laugh. 'But sure God himself couldn't put an oul head on young shoulders. Nor soften a young cock.' A sigh; a sip. 'Still, it's an awful shame. A young fellow like you, with the world at your feet. What age are you, Teddy?'

'Twenty-six.'

'Twenty-six! God-oh-God! If I could be twenty-six again, knowing what I know at eighty – ' He broke off with a laugh. 'Do you know, Teddy, I'd do it all again. The selfsame way. But' – he sipped his whiskey – 'ah, if only I could be a young man again.'

Teddy sneaked a look at his uncle. He felt suddenly like crying. His life was before him, for all it was worth; he didn't want it. If he could, he'd gladly change places with Con.

Con sipped again. 'Still, I've no quarrel with God – if there is a God. But if he stops me at the gate above, and says to try my luck below, I'll give him what I gave Lamarr!' He laughed again. Fierce. Defiant. Loud.

Teddy was feeling strange in his head. But not weepy any more: a dull confusing anger. Was everyone's life as pointless as his? As cruel as Con's?

'Did I ever tell you about Lamarr?'

Teddy shook his head. Surely his life was worth more than this? To be sure, there were men who had more than porridge and spuds to eat, and who could put their hand on what belonged to them at night. Why couldn't he be one of them? And why did Con . . .?

'Lamarr was the biggest man on the boat.' Con began the story of the fight the way he always did. 'The first boat I ever sailed in, out of Liverpool. I was nineteen. Not a man jack on the seven seas but didn't know Meadie Lamarr. Not a man jack but didn't walk aisy round him. He was bigger than yourself. Six foot four, with a head and shoulders on him like a bull. He'd killed two men in Rio with his bare hands . . .'

The strange confusing angry feeling in Teddy's head went away of a sudden. Of a sudden he was sure of something as he had never been sure of anything in his life: Uncle Con was dying; he would never see him again. He reached for his porter. It was half drunk. There was a froth-furred glass beside it, and he was surprised to realise he'd emptied that. Another, full – whose was that? The barman was leaning with his elbows on the bar, listening, that dirty smirk on him, and Teddy had the notion to go over and bury his fist up to the wrist beneath the black moustache.

It was quiet in the bar. More than the barman was listening to the tale.

'Hey boy!' Teddy called. 'You might make yourself useful.' He glared around him. Conversation struck up at the tables and the bar.

The barman brought more drink. 'Go on,' Teddy muttered. The barman went away. Con supped his whiskey.

'Anyway: there he was, looking at me like a mastiff, and me pissing myself, and next thing he calls me an Irish bastard. Begod the blood got up in me then! No man calls me a bastard! says I, and I jumped to my feet and faced him. And this was Meadie Lamarr, mind. Well I'm calling one now! says he.'

Con's voice had risen to a reedy screech. Again the bar was silent.

'There was three blows struck, Teddy. My hand and word to God. The blow I hit him on the jaw, the blow his skull hit the bulkhead, and the blow he hit the deck when he came down. It shook the ship! And do you know, before we were rightly across the Atlantic, we were the best of friends.'

Teddy shook the death's grip off his arm and struggled to his feet.

'What the hell are yous all gawking at!' he bellowed. The farmers and dealers quickly turned back to their own affairs and began to murmur. The barman opened his mouth but shut it when Teddy looked at him. 'It's the truth!'

'Sit down, Teddy. Sit down,' Con said softly.

Teddy set his chair back on its legs and did as he was bidden. He sniffed ferociously.

A man barged through the door, a red-haired young fellow. 'Hey,' he shouted. 'There's a war on!'

'Is it only now you're learning that?' the barman scoffed.

There was a general snicker of laughter. Con joined in.

A man sidled over from the bar and spoke to them. 'Amn't I the sorry man didn't know that when I set out this morning!' He looked mournful and none too sober. 'A grand six-quarter filly I had to sell. Took forty pounds for her on the road coming in at eight o'clock, from a robber of a guinea-man. Thought I was made up. Thought the man was drunk. I could have got a hundred on the fairgreen at nine.'

Teddy stared at him. The man went out the back. Con followed.

How much? Teddy wondered. He reached his hand into his pocket and the half-crown there was hot from his blood. Handing money to his mother had been one thing, but to his mother-in-law it would be another. All he had to show for all he'd saved before his marriage was a pisspot and a plough, and a bed he slept in with his wife's oul man. The sovereigns and silver that remained were in a bag beneath the other mattress. It was his wife who would pay for the seed in O'Hare's.

'Sure when ye've money enough saved up we can build our own wee room, Teddy.' He sneered at the recollection of Lizzie-Ann's wheedling explanation – be a long time, wouldn't it? 'But I couldn't sleep in the same bed as you' – giggling madly – 'in the same room with me ma! Sure you can sleep with Da until the time comes.'

Dan didn't grumble. The double bed was better than the settlebed, which had been better than the hay-bed in the loft. Dan was coming up rightly in the world, bechrist! Dan was doing well.

Jaysus wasn't porter powerful stuff! Teddy signalled for another, and a whiskey for Con.

'What time's the train?' he asked of two men seated at a nearby table. They broke off their haggling and one, a ruddy-faced dealer in gaiters and corduroy britches, gave him a peevish look. The other, leathery-looking and muddy, frowned attentively.

'The Dublin train?' he asked.

'Eh – aye.'

'There's one at half-past two, I think,' the dealer said busily. 'There's one at six o'clock.'

'Thanks.'

Con returned. 'I was talking to that fellow out the back, but he was manthog drunk.' He raised his voice. 'Who's fighting?'

No one answered. Teddy locked eyes with the barman.

'Who's fighting – damn your skins! In the war?'

'Germany, I think,' the red-headed young fellow said.

'And England?'

'Eh – I think so.'

'Well here's to the Kaiser!' Con roared, and raised his glass.

There was a low guffaw. Someone answered the toast, and arguments commenced.

'A war, begod!' Con said, marvelling. 'I was never in a war.' Then he was silent, and when Teddy looked the old eyes were fixed on him. 'A war'll make the country up, you know. Make us all up. They'll be looking for recruits.' He lowered his voice. 'Now's your chance, Teddy. Last one you'll get.'

Teddy felt his face flush again. His uncle had read his thoughts. 'Ach – I'd be no good at fighting.'

'You only think that, gasún. Wait till you see when the blood gets up in you. Do you think I'd have taken a pension to face Meadie Lamarr?'

'I'm no fighter,' Teddy muttered. 'I'm not like you.'

'Aha, lad, you're more like me than you think. Closest to a son I ever had. Ever knew, anyway!' Con chuckled.

'I'm no fighter,' Teddy said again – gruffly, blinking hard. 'I'm – I'm not like you, Uncle Con.'

'D'ye tell me, now! And d'ye tell me you weren't facing up to carry the head off yon cheeky scut of a barman a while ago?'

Teddy said nothing.

Con sipped his whiskey. 'Even so, even so. A war's a good time to make a break for it – best chance you'll ever get. The world's full of places you could hide. And who'll have time to look for you? Aye, places. Australia's there, wide open since I left! Canada, Alasky, South America. Full of places.' He jerked on Teddy's arm, and stared into his eyes. 'And I've still that ten pounds. Ten sovereigns in gold. Like I told you at the wedding. And they're still yours if you'll go. I'll give you them tonight, as soon as we get home. All I've left out of two sheep stations and half a ship, but ten pounds more than I had when I struck out. Had to hide them up me hole on the trek across the Gibson, but I washed them since, and you're more than welcome to them, *gasún*. Because you're the best of them. You're a man like myself though you mightn't know it, and I'd do anything to see you get another chance.' He drained his glass. 'They can bury me a pauper. I won't care.'

'I don't need them, Con.'

For a moment anger flared, but Teddy held the wicked gaze, and the old face crinkled and Con let go of him and leaned back in his chair and laughed.

'No! Begod you don't! Horses going for a hundred pounds' – he grasped Teddy's arm again – 'and you owe them nothing!

'I'm going out the back,' he said then. 'These wee things only hold so much at my age.' He cackled and stood up. Teddy did the same, unsmiling. He put out his hand. Con took it. He squeezed it hard with both of his, and stared into his nephew's eyes. His own were dim and moist.

'God go with you, *a mhic*. If I was twenty years younger I'd go with you myself. If I was twenty – twenty-six again, knowing what I know at eighty – ach, but what's the use of talking! I'd do it all again. The selfsame way. There's none of us has any choice.'

At the back door he turned. 'Mind yourself.'

Teddy finished his drink, went to the bar, and demanded his change. He got a sixpence and a few coppers, and he dropped the coppers into his pocket on top of the half-crown. He felt their chill on his leg through the cloth. He tossed the tanner back.

'And two more whiskeys.' The barman set a glass before him. 'Two, I said.'

'That's a double.'

Teddy got a good grip of the front of the white shirt and hauled the barman halfway over the bar. The smirk fell off the pale face – paler now. The pub was as quiet as a church at consecration. Teddy stared into the wide dark frightened eyes.

'If I hear tell you said a word to him, one unmannerly word, I'll come back and I'll bre'k your neck.' He let go of the shirt, walked to the corner, placed the whiskey on the table, and stepped back to the bar. 'You're not fit to lace his boots.'

In the fresh air, the street was swaying, his feet hitting the cobbled pavement each a little sooner than he was expecting. Outside the hardware shop he untied the Clydesdale and led it off. The ploughslide was still hanging from the hames, and it swung with every step the horse took at his back and struck the collar, and he heard the soft thump of the steel against the straw-stuffed leather for the first time. Somewhere up the street the legless lunatic was raving. 'Help Lord Kitchener! A penny for Lord Kitchener!'

The Angelus bells were ringing as the big hoofs were muffled by the fairgreen's turf. Lizzie-Ann would be waiting – to hell with her. There was a man in army uniform shouting, and Teddy went up to him. Without a word the army man examined the horse. He looked in its mouth and peeled each eyelid back. He ran two firm hands down each leg, and lifted each hoof and the tail in turn, and poked and explored. He took four strides back and gauged the animal from the rear, then went in front and did the same from there. He watched as another soldier trotted the horse off and back again, closing one eye and squinting between the hairy legs as if along a gun.

'Name?' he said, pulling a notebook from a pocket. He had the same accent as the gaitered man in the bar, throaty and thick, and he sounded like he meant business.

'I'm only asking,' Teddy murmured.

'Hey!' he heard the army dealer call behind him. 'Hey you! Come back here.'

Teddy turned and faced him.

'I'll give you fifty quid.'

'I'm not selling.'

'What about fifty-five?'

'He's not for sale.'

The army dealer shrugged and put his notebook back.

In a corner of the green there was a young fellow in a patched tweed jacket, no older than himself. A total stranger. Teddy trusted him on sight. The young fellow offered fifty pounds. They settled on sixty-five, spat on their palms and shook. The young fellow gave another quid for the harness, even though, as he said, the British ordnance supplied its own. Sixty-six pounds in paper and silver and gold. Teddy stuffed the money into his pocket on top of the half-crown and the coppers. He made a luck-penny of the chit for the plough.

'What time's the next train?' he asked.

'Half-two, I think. To Dublin?'

Teddy was already walking. He knew where the train station was. The Clydesdale nickered anxiously after him, and he looked over his shoulder and saw the long blazed face up high, the ears cocked forward, the eyes behind the blinkers watching him. He felt a shiver of guilt and unease. But he didn't break stride. Half-two. He'd be in Dublin before he was missed. There was a boat to Liverpool, where Uncle Con had joined the navy – but no, there was a war on. In Liverpool they might pick him up and force him into the army. They might send him back here or to jail. He didn't want to fight with anyone. From Dublin he could catch another train to Cork. From Queenstown, Uncle Con had often told him, there were boats leaving every week. For Canada, America, Australia.

Lizzie-Ann would be outside Saint Nicholas's, so Teddy went round by the Marist. He caught the reek of boiling cabbage at the Square, and paused and touched the money bulging in his pocket. He went into the eating house and took his cap off. A man he knew eyed him curiously over a forkful of boiled bacon. Teddy pretended not to see him. The hands of the clock on the wall made a shape he wasn't sure of, and he asked the lassie who poured tea for him the time.

'Going on for one.'

Plenty o' time. Too much of it, maybe. The man was coming over, grease glistening on his whiskers.

'Teddy, begod! I thought it looked like you.'

'Well George.' George Butler, Lizzie-Ann's uncle – his own now, by marriage.

'Times must be good,' Butler remarked, 'if young fellows can eat in town.'

'Aye,' Teddy answered, the strange feeling still in his head. 'It's good times for us all. The Kaiser's at war with – with England.'

'So I hear, so I hear.' A pause. 'Good times for young fellows anyway. Were you selling stock?'

'No. Just doing a message for Dan. But the horse lost a shoe coming in. I'm getting him shod.'

'With Cunningham?'

'Eh – aye.'

'I suppose. And there's plenty in front of you, I suppose?'

'No shortage. Fair days is busy days for blacksmiths.'

'O' course, o' course.' Teddy felt the man's eyes on him. He sipped his tea. 'Good times is right. Good times for young fellows anyway, that has the price of a shoeing *and* a big feed in their pockets.'

'It's my money. My own money I'm spending.'

'Oh I'm sure it is. Who else's would you be spending? But it's bloody well for you, is all I can say, has the price of a shoeing *and* a big feed in your pocket. I couldn't have done it, when I was your age. Where's the money coming from at all!'

'It's the war,' Teddy muttered. 'Good times for Ireland at last.'

'Dambut-skin, man, sure the war's only started! I only heard this morning on the fairgreen.'

'Were you selling?'

'No,' Butler said, drawing out the word. 'But I'll be selling next time. Now's the time to sell' – Teddy could feel the eyes burning into him – 'if you've anything to sell.'

The lassie brought the feed. Butler took himself off.

Teddy ate the spuds and bacon, left the cabbage on his plate, and drank the milky tea. Sitting at the table, he felt lonely more than scared. He'd miss Uncle Con, and he'd miss his ma. Hard to think he'd never see either of them again. He'd miss his sisters and his brothers. He'd even miss old Dan.

He'd write a letter home some day. Some day soon, before Con died. Ma could read it to him.

From where? he wondered. Queensland, Quebec? – names Con had mentioned. Nicaragua, New Zealand, the Nullarbor? – names that were strange and exciting. He was big and broad and the food soaked up the porter in his belly and before he finished he could taste the tea. Outside, his feet were steady on the cobbles, and his ankles firm beneath him, and he walked the length of Park Street without looking to the left or to the right or to the rear. A motor car chugged past, but he hardly noticed. If George Butler clapped a hand on him, he'd carry the head off his neck with a thump, and take his chances.

But there was no sign of Butler, and no policemen at the station. Teddy stood close to the ticket window with the peak of his cap over his eyes and shoved his money over. He hid in the toilet till he heard the train pull in.

Lizzie-Ann was waiting on the platform.

'Aha!' she crowed, 'just like George said. What did you do with my father's horse?'

Teddy's face was flying off him. People were staring. They began to stop. 'Nothing,' he muttered. 'He's below at the forge in Carrolls' Yard getting shod.'

'He is in me arse! George checked that lie out. He's going round the fairgreen now to see if he can find him. You sold him, didn't you? Didn't you, you thieving get!'

A big grey-whiskered man came over. 'What's the matter, missus?' He glared at Teddy.

'Aw, what's the matter? This fellow's after stealing my father's horse, and now he's leaving me. And me in the family way.' She began to sniffle.

'Is that right?' the big man said fiercely.

'No, no.' The big man sniffed. 'It was my own horse,' Teddy said. 'I – I did a deal with her father.' The big man sniffed again, then took a quick step back.

'He's a liar!' Lizzie-Ann screeched. 'He never did.'

The big man walked away. Someone spoke to him. 'Pair of drunk tinkers' – Teddy heard the reply. The man got on the train. The crowd began to thin.

'Get a policeman,' Lizzie-Ann called. The platform was almost empty, though eyes were staring from the carriages. Teddy took a step. 'You're not leaving me?' she cried. 'Me that'll have your child before Christmas?'

'You'll have it long before then.' She looked at him; she reddened. 'There's nobody belonging to me in there.'

'Such a dirty thing to say!' She started to bawl. Teddy stepped round her. She grabbed his arm. 'You can't leave me, Teddy?'

They were the only ones on the platform now, apart from a few gawking porters. Suddenly Teddy felt awfully sorry for her.

'I'm – I'm just going to join the army. They pay great money. I'll send it home to you.'

A shrewd look flitted across her face, but only for a moment. A whistle blew. The sound of the engine changed.

'No, no! You're only saying that. You were talking to that oul daftie of an uncle of yours. 'Twas him put the bad notion in your head to leave me.'

The train began to move. A cloud of steam and coal-smoke filled Teddy's nostrils. He felt frantic. He tried to thrust her away. But she held on. Desperate, he dug one hand into his pocket and pulled out a fistful of treasury notes. A coin fell onto the platform with the solid clang of gold and rolled under the train.

'Here,' he said, moving, dragging her along with him. 'That's what I got for the horse. Give it to Dan. The war'll be over by Christmas, he can buy another cheap then.'

She took the money but held onto his arm. The train was picking up speed. He shoved her – hard – and ran.

'No! No, come back here.'

But Teddy was running, faster than she could. He grabbed a carriage doorhandle, tugged and twisted. Over his wife's screams he heard a male voice roar at him in rage. He twisted the handle again. The door swung open – against him – threw him back. The train was going fast now. Teddy ran his hardest. He got abreast of the doorway again – but he'd reached the end of the platform. An arm reached out. He made a despairing leap, his eyes on the slicing wheels. A strong hand grasped his wrist and jerked him inside.

'Cut it a bit fine, didn't you?' A youngish man in a tweed suit was grinning at him, still holding his wrist. Teddy mumbled thanks.

He found a carriage with a disappointed dealer in it, well drunk, muttering and grumbling. The drooling mouth and open bottle and the stench of horse-dunged boots had kept out the women with their awl-sharp eyes and butcher-knife minds, and Teddy kept his cap pulled down and didn't look at any of the curious, silent men. He was shaking. He hoped he'd done the right thing. Though he didn't doubt it. He'd miss them all, even his wife – but Con would soon be dead, and this was the way he'd wanted it. And there would be other women out there. Aye, no shortage. Women in every port. Other places. The world was full of them. Perth and San Francisco. Cape Horn and Batumi. Black cannibals, and girls without a stitch on them but bits of grass. The Gibson Desert, and gold every time you shat.

The conductor came and punched his ticket. Teddy stopped shaking. He was big and strong and young, and had it all before him. Places, places, places, places – the wheels of the train were chanting him away. Suez and Mombasa and the Virgin Islands. Sydney and Ceylon and Singapore. He had fifty years ahead of him before he need come home to die. Cape Horn and Corpus Christi and Constantinople. He'd see them all, as Con had seen them, all them places. The Arctic Ocean, the China Sea, the Great Australian Bight. The world was full of places. He had it at his feet. If he could learn to ride a horse he was its master.

FICTION

from

THE BLACKSTAFF PRESS

THE ROAD TO NOTOWN
A NOVEL

·

MICHAEL FOLEY

A scurrilous, brilliantly satirical novel about the pretensions, hypocrisies and paranoia of the literary world and its hangers-on – novelists, poets, academics, passionate women and barking-mad eccentrics – and, for good measure, Northern Irish cultural conditioning, marital breakdown and the maelstrom that passes for family life.

'a wonderful book full of epigrammatic wit, scatalogical delight, comic invention, I'm sure, and, no doubt, truth'

LEON McAULEY, *FORTNIGHT*

'viciously hilarious tale'

KENNETH WRIGHT, *GLASGOW HERALD*

'the most enjoyable comic book I have read recently'

LAR CASSIDY, *IRISH TIMES*

pb; 198 x 129 mm; 352 pp; £7.99
0-85640-576-0

BREAKING OUT
A NOVEL

·

AISLING MAGUIRE

Eleanor Leyden is a rebel, a 'girl that spells trouble'. When her communist parents are killed in the car crash which also leaves her maimed, she is fostered by family friends, Dermot and Angela O'Driscoll. But as she grows up, she feels increasingly stifled by their middle-class Catholic values. Bursting into 'defiant flame', she rejects their conservative world as she becomes a stone-mason and seeks solace in a forbidden love affair that only further entraps her.

Two women inspire her flight – her outspoken Aunt Katherine and her precocious schoolfriend Louise. With Louise she discovers the 'exhilaration of departure' as they travel to France and Greece. Here, when their intense bond shifts from warm banter to sexual rivalry and desire, Eleanor learns that she must face the world 'herself, clear, alone'.

'Aisling Maguire delves deep into the psyche of her emotionally powerful central character. The result is a dynamic insight into the background forces that steer the course of all our lives ... an author whose follow-up novel will be eagerly awaited by all.'

SOPHIE GORMÁN, *IRISH INDEPENDENT*

'authentic dialogue ... highly readable'

KATIE DONOVAN, *IRISH TIMES*

pb; 198 x 129 mm; 208 pp; £6.99
0-85640-574-4

BOOING THE BISHOP
AND OTHER STORIES

·

JUDE COLLINS

Revolving around Jimmy Rice, a young boy growing up in 1950s Derry and Omagh, *Booing the Bishop and Other Stories* is a poignant – and sometimes pungent – evocation of a Catholic upbringing. Thundering fire-and-brimstone priests and strap-happy Christian Brothers do constant battle with their 'shameless, sacrilegious guttersnipe' pupils; a boy prays to Saint Patrick for a 'hot coort'; and a relic of Saint Bernadette is traded for a glimpse of a girl's 'b.t.m.'. This is the time of Saturday matinées with Roy Rogers, 'Peggy Sue' on the jukebox and 'corner boys larded with Brylcreem' furtively puffing Gallaher's Blues as they dream of being Marlon Brando.

Warmly and closely observed, Jude Collins's riotous characters – Presumer Livingstone, Snots Casey, Nipper McGrath, Bubbles McCann – caper through a world where their animal high spirits and sexual curiosity keep them on a collision course with the sensibilities and pomposities of the adults in charge of them. Fresh and pacy tales from a writer with a keen eye and an even keener ear – and a sure sense of how to coax the last ounce of fun out of a great story.

'[Collins] has an unsurpassed gift for capturing the brave and wild talk of 11-year-olds. The stories are taut, economical and funny, and never put a foot wrong.'

CAREY HARRISON, *IRISH TIMES*

pb; 198 x 129 mm; 144 pp; £5.99
0-85640-567-1

SAM HANNA BELL

·

DECEMBER BRIDE

The classic novel of Ulster life, now a major film.

'not just a remarkable artistic achievement, but also a remarkable political one . . . opens up a community's sense of itself, restoring a richness and complexity to a history that has been deliberately narrowed'

FINTAN O'TOOLE, *IRISH TIMES*
REVIEWING THE FILM *DECEMBER BRIDE*

'a story of the eternal triangle, held, like the land, by stubborn force'

FORTNIGHT

'invested with a disquieting and sullen beauty'

SATURDAY REVIEW OF LITERATURE

pb; 214 x 137 mm; 304 pp; £5.95
0-85640-061-0

ERIN'S ORANGE LILY and SUMMER LOANEN

Two classics from Sam Hanna Bell in one volume.

'an informal and delightful ramble through Ulster folkways, from the Orange Walk and the making of poteen to bargaining at country fairs and the etiquette of dealing with the fairy folk'

KENNETH WRIGHT, *GLASGOW HERALD*

pb; 198 x 129 mm; 224 pp; £7.99
0-85640-589-2

ORDERING BLACKSTAFF BOOKS

All Blackstaff Press books are available through bookshops. In the case of difficulty, however, orders can be made directly to Gill & Macmillan UK Distribution, Blackstaff's distributor. Indicate clearly the title and number of copies required and send order with your name and address to:

CASH SALES

Gill & Macmillan UK Distribution
13–14 Goldenbridge Industrial Estate
Inchicore
Dublin 8

Please enclose a remittance to the value of the cover price plus: £2.50 for the first book plus 50p per copy for each additional book ordered to cover postage and packing.
Payment should be made in sterling by UK personal cheque, sterling draft or international money order, made payable to Gill & Macmillan UK Distribution; or by MasterCard or Visa.

Please debit my MasterCard* Visa* account
*Cross out which is inapplicable

My card number is (13 or 16 digits)

Signature

Expiry date

Name on card

Address

Applicable only in the UK and Republic of Ireland

Full catalogue available on request from
The Blackstaff Press Limited
3 Galway Park, Dundonald, Belfast BT16 0AN
Northern Ireland
Tel. 01232 487161; Fax 01232 489552;
e-mail books@blkstaff.dnet.co.uk